Praise for the work of Edgar-winner Ruth Birmingham and ace Atlanta PI Sunny Childs

"Witty, irreverent."—Harlan Coben, author of *Fade Away*

"Top-notch . . . the further adventures of Sunny Childs will be most welcome."   —*Booklist*

"Ruth Birmingham has established herself as the Queen of Atlanta crime fiction. Read and enjoy."
            —Fred Willard, author of *Down on Ponce*

"Gets better with each installment."
            —*Fort Lauderdale Sun-Sentinel*

"Sunny Childs is . . . a wham-bam-thank-you-ma'am great read."   —J. A. Jance, author of *Name Withheld*

COLD TRAIL

RUTH BIRMINGHAM

BERKLEY PRIME CRIME, NEW YORK

COLD TRAIL

A Berkley Prime Crime Book / published by arrangement with the author

PRINTING HISTORY
Berkley Prime Crime mass-market edition / September 2002

Visit our website at
www.penguinputnam.com

ISBN: 0-425-18273-8

Berkley Prime Crime Books are published
by The Berkley Publishing Group,
a division of Penguin Putnam Inc.,
375 Hudson Street, New York, New York 10014.
The name BERKLEY PRIME CRIME and the BERKLEY PRIME CRIME
design are trademarks belonging to Penguin Putnam Inc.

PRINTED IN THE UNITED STATES OF AMERICA

10   9   8   7   6   5   4   3   2   1

CHAPTER 1

BECAUSE THE ASSIGNMENT demanded it, I was driving a car I'd borrowed from my mother, a Jag that cost more than I'd paid for the place where I live. It handled marvelously, accelerated like a dream, and the heater didn't work worth crap. So the goddamn windows fogged up and I couldn't see a goddamn thing, and at five goddamn minutes after midnight I ran off the road and hit a goddamn tree.

I was not in the mood, thanks.

I was somewhere in the middle of the poorest, most backward, most pathetic county in Georgia, in the middle of a trackless and interminable forest of plantation pine pulpwood, on a road that didn't appear on any map, driving toward an assignment I did not want to be doing, and one word kept buzzing through my brain like a crazy bee: Goddamn. Goddamn, goddamn, goddamn.

And then, like that, as though a switch had been thrown, the tires on the wonderfully grippy Jag lost traction and—WHAM—I was looking at the trunk of a pine tree, cracks spiderwebbing across my windshield, the air bag deflating in my lap.

I climbed out of the car, and said to the dark nowhere, "So. Could this get any goddamn goddamn
goddamn goddamn goddamn worse?" At which point,
a bolt of lightning hit the tree under which I was standing. It was as though a sun had gone supernova in my
head. When I came to, I was lying fifteen feet from
the car in the driving rain and my mouth was full of
water. Which is when I stopped being pissed at Gunnar
Brushwood and my mother, and started getting scared.

"Hey," Gunnar had said earlier in the week. "It's just
a bunch of old rich ladies who have a lodge in the
country. Some old gal died there last year, you poke
around a little, you send them a nice fat bill, they pay
it with a check from one of the banks their husbands
own. Simple. What could go wrong?"

I had explained that I had several extremely good
reasons for not wanting to take the assignment. At
which point Gunnar had showed me the check they'd
written us. It was, as they say, sizeable. "Then again,"
I'd said, "maybe I could clear my calendar . . ."

It took me half an hour, jamming brush under the
wheels, rocking the car back and forth, great fonts of
cursing erupting to the skies, and the utter destruction
of my sixteen-hundred-dollar cashmere ensemble, to
get the car rolling again.

Which only put me back where I had been—lost in
the wilderness of rural Georgia at one o'clock in the
morning, angry, cold, scared, hungry.

Oh, yeah, and the gas tank was on Empty.

I had only one headlight now and it pointed down
at the ground at such an acute angle that I could see

only about twenty feet in front of me, so I went creeping down the two-lane highway in the direction I'd come. The window fogged up again, so I had to roll down the window, letting the rain pour in on me. The cold frigid icy *freezing-ass* rain. Just in case I hadn't made that clear. It was November, and the temperature outside was in the mid-thirties. Soon I was shivering uncontrollably.

The occasional flash of lightning served only to tell me what I already knew, that I was in the middle of a forest of planted pine, every tree exactly the same height, the same shape, the same size—the trunks disappearing into the black distance on all sides. No houses, no fences, no farms, no cars, no nothing.

Finally I came to a road sign. Which was lying flat on the ground after apparently having been run over by some yokel in a monster truck. After getting out of the car and yanking the sign upright, I was able to determine that Hightower, Georgia, a sad little ruin of a town I'd driven through earlier in the night, was seven miles away. But—again, thank you thank you thank you very goddamn much, Mr. Monster-truck-driving-yokel—a spray of bullet holes in the sign made it impossible to say whether Hightower was to the right or the left. I took the left fork. Ten minutes later, I was still creeping through the woods. An orange light on the dash began flashing and from some hidden orifice a voice with a snotty British accent began intoning, "You are almost out of fuel. You are almost out of fuel. You are almost out of . . ."

I turned around and drove back the way I'd come. At the fork, I went the other way. It was now nearing two o'clock and my fingers were so cold I couldn't feel the steering wheel.

Suddenly I saw something. Back in the woods: a light. Then two. Two feeble lights bobbing up and down. I pulled the car over and jumped out.

"Hey!" I yelled. "Hey! Help!"

Then I heard the sound, a dreadful baying or screaming coming out of the woods.

"Hey!"

There was more screaming, barely audible through the thunder and the driving rain. But the two lights seemed to turn, hesitate, move toward me.

"Hey!"

The awful noise, the screaming or whatever it was, rose and fell and the two lights kept bobbing toward me, like ghostly apparitions in the night. Sometimes they would disappear for a moment, flicker, then reappear. The screaming grew louder. For a moment I considered getting back in the car and driving away, but I was so cold and numb that I felt rooted to the spot, as though I were mesmerized.

And then the two lights appeared out of the gloom and became human figures, barely distinguishable against the black trees.

"Hello?" I said.

It was only then that I was able to see that they were men, men wearing miner's lights on their heads. The two lights were aimed at me, glaring in my eyes, so that the faces of the two men were just invisible smears of black against the deeper darkness of the night.

"You ort not to be out here, lady," one of the men said. He had a deep country accent. There was something twisted about his frame, as though he'd been picked up by a giant and pinched almost in half.

"No shit," I said.

The other man said, "She got a mouth on her, don't she?" The way he said it didn't sound friendly.

"Look, I'm sorry, I'm trying to find the Hellespont Lodge. I wrecked my car."

The two lights swiveled toward my mother's car. "Jaguar," the twisted man said. "That's one them foreign cars, ain't it?"

Behind them I could still hear the eerie screaming. "What's that noise?" I said.

"That's the hounds."

"They don't sound like any dogs I've ever heard."

"Tracking us a prisoner. Some boy excaped from over to the penitentiary."

"Oh. Great."

The man wiped his face with his arm. "Dogs can't even get no scent in this rain. I don't even know why we botherin'."

"You don't want to be stopping," the second man said. "Nor picking up nobody."

The light on the first man's head shook back and forth. "Nope. You don't even want to be *talking* to nobody. Night like this?"

"Any damn thing could happen."

The lights moved a step or two closer, slid up and down my body. "*Any* damn thing."

"I'm sure that's true," I said. "But can you tell me how to get to the Hellespont Lodge?"

The two men eased another step closer. I could feel their eyes on my body. "You don't want to go to no Hellespont Lodge," the twisted man said.

"Huh-uh." The second light swept back and forth in

agreement. "Some rich lady got kilt over there last year."

The first light bobbed up and down. "Ay-uh. Skinny gal, 'bout like you but taller. Had a big ol' hole right there in her th'oat. My cousin Jerry Hayden—Jerry with the missing foot, not fat Jerry—he showed her to me 'fore she got took to the autopsy. I ever tell you that, Roy?"

"Hell, no, you never did. He showed you a *dead* lady? Dadgum!"

I was getting nervous. "I just need directions, guys."

The two edged toward me another step or two. Behind them the screaming pack of dogs—I could hear now that was what it was—was beginning to grow closer.

The two flashlights turned back toward the woods. "He must of doubled back, Roy."

"Ay-uh. He might could of did."

"Might be anydamnwher around here."

"Guys?" I said. My teeth were chattering. "Guys, please, could you just give me directions?"

The storm seemed to slacken and for a moment the entire world grew quiet. One of the lights swept to my left, pointing back the way I'd come. "It's back yunder, the way you come."

"Hard to see it," the other man said. "The entrance is got all overgrowed. Don't much of nobody go there no more."

" 'Bout a mile, mile and a half back."

Then lightning flashed and for the first time I saw a brief flash of their faces. One man's toothless mouth was open and slack. The other man was so thin that his face looked like the rictus grin of a skull. The thunder crashed as I screamed.

Then I was back in the Jag, flooring it about two seconds later, my wheels throwing mud into the air.

Out the window I heard one of the men's voices, nearly swallowed up in the rain: "The hail's wrong with *her*?"

In front of me I could see almost nothing. I continued to accelerate, even though I couldn't see where I was going. Suddenly there was a black blur moving in front of the car. I slammed on my brakes but it was too late. I saw a flash of white shirt with a black stripe down the side. Prison uniform. There was a thump as I hit him with the bumper, a second thump as he banged into the windshield and spun over the top of the car.

I floored it and didn't look back.

Sure enough I had missed the entrance the first time. It was a sign about the size of a loaf of bread that simply read HELLESPONT. I turned onto the rutted track and began driving. For a few hundred yards it was gravel, but then the gravel yielded to mud. The car was balking occasionally, sliding from side to side, the engine coughing and sputtering. The light saying I was out of gas continued to flash.

Then suddenly I broke out of the woods and into a brushy clearing.

There, at the top of the hill, was the lodge, a dark brooding pile of a building. It appeared, for a moment in a flash of lightning, then returned to the darkness. The place reminded me, in that brief flash, of a ruined castle.

I kept driving. The lodge disappeared from view as

I went back into a stand of trees that wound circuitously up the hill. Then suddenly, there in front of me, stood a man, holding a kerosene lantern in his hand. His eyes were black, piercing, unsettling; his long black hair was plastered to his head by the rain.

A thought flashed through me mind: *well, at least he isn't an escaped prisoner.* At which point the Jag gave a final bucking rattle and ceased to operate altogether.

I stuck my head out the window. "Is this the lodge?" I yelled.

The man didn't answer, just stared at me with his creepy black eyes. I was not comforted by the large hunting knife he carried in a cross-draw sheath on his belt.

"My car!" I yelled. "I think it's out of gas."

He continued to stare. I could see the lodge up ahead, so I hopped out of the car, my feet unable to feel the ground now. I tried to open the trunk of my Jaguar, but I couldn't hold my keys with my frozen fingers. The creepy man came up beside me, grabbed the keys from my hand, opened the trunk, and pulled out my Louis Vuitton bag and the case I carried my bow and arrows in. The Vuitton suitcase must have weighed forty pounds, but the man carried it effortlessly as he began trudging through the rain up to the dark lodge.

We entered through a huge oak door, which groaned on its massive wrought iron hinges. He set the bags down in the lobby. It was a vast, cold room with a huge stone fireplace in which the last few embers of a meager fire burned.

"Where do I go?" I said. "Do I have a room or something?"

But the creepy man didn't answer. Instead he walked back out the groaning door and disappeared into the rain and the darkness.

I sat down in an old leather chair in front of the pitiful fire and began to shake like a leaf.

CHAPTER 2

I HAD HALFWAY collected myself when I heard a noise. Standing over me was a tall redhead of Rubenesque proportions. She wore a funereal black robe which hung to the floor, and carried a black candelabrum. In the flickering candlelight, her eyes looked black and piercing.

"Oh. My. God." She had a deep, drawling voice that spoke of cigarettes and old Southern money. "Look at *you*, little baby."

I recognized the voice: it was my client, Martha Herrington. Or, as she had referred to herself on the phone, Mrs. Dale Herrington IV.

I tried to stand, but I could hardly get up.

"What in the name of heaven happened to you?"

My teeth were still chattering and my face was so frozen I could hardly talk. All that came out of my mouth was, "Wreck. Lost. Hit something. Road. Agh." Or something similarly unintelligible.

She stared with her piercing black eyes. "You *are* Sunny Childs, aren't you?"

I nodded. After that I'm not quite sure what happened. I remember being supported by two people while stumbling up a flight of flagstone stairs. Also I was aware of being watched by many eyes. It took me a while to suss out the fact that I was being watched, not by people, but by the glass eyes of various dead beasts which hung on the high stone walls of the lodge.

And then Mrs. Dale Herrington the fourth was gone and I was submerged in an old clawfoot tub full of hot water, being scrubbed and kneaded by the hands of a woman with bloodlessly pale skin, pale blue eyes, hair the color of cornsilk, and large mannish powerful hands. I was so tired and cold that I didn't even feel nonplussed by this peculiar invasion of my personal space. At that moment, hot water seemed worth the price of any indignity.

Like the man who picked up my bags, the bloodless woman didn't speak. But there was something about her, some aspect of her bearing or manner, that made her seem not to be an American.

I may have fallen asleep briefly as I was being ministered to by the bloodless woman, but then I was awake again, standing naked in the middle of the old-fashioned bathroom, being dried with a very expensive-feeling towel, and then clothed in a pair of silk pajamas and a green silk robe with a monogram on it.

"I think I need to go to sleep," I said vaguely. "Where's my room?"

The bloodless woman motioned me to follow her. In her hand she carried a candlestick, which lit our way down the stone-walled passageway. The flickering light gave the place an eerie atmosphere. I followed her down the flight of steps I had climbed earlier. She motioned to a chair in front of the fireplace. Someone had built it up so that it blazed brightly. But still, in the huge room its heat and light were both swallowed by the chill and the gloom.

"Where's my room, please?" I said. A little more sharply this time.

The woman didn't answer. Instead she began walking down a passage leading toward the back of the building, leaving me in semidarkness.

"Hey!" I said. "Hey, hold on."

But like the creepy man earlier, she simply ignored me and disappeared into the gloom.

I was beginning to curse my boss, when Martha Herrington appeared at the top of the stairs again, still carrying the large black candelabrum. She was looking down at me curiously.

"Did Uma not show you your room?" she said.

I shook my head.

She clucked loudly, made a face of exaggerated annoyance. "That *woman*. I am *so* sorry, Sunny, my gosh, I don't *even* know what to say. These krauts are efficient, but—my stars!—they do not have the least *notion* of hospitality." She glided down the stairs, her robe billowing around her. "Welcome to Hellespont Lodge."

I tried to smile. I was now pretty warm, but I was still put out, still exhausted, still feeling emotionally beat-up from the events of the night.

"I know you want to get your little tootsies into a nice warm bed, honey," Martha Herrington said, "but since you're here and we're by our lonesomes, I just want to get a few things straight so this all goes as planned." She smiled a sort of smile that Southern women use when speaking to the help, and her voice dropped slightly. "And of course, I need to set a few ground rules."

"Can it wait?" I said.

"Oh, this won't take any time at all," she said brightly. "Let's go this way."

I followed her resignedly as she swept down a dark hallway leading out of the back of the entry hall.

"I *do* apologize for the primitiveness of the conditions and all this folderol." She held up her candelabrum. "But what you will discover about us is that we hold fast to all sorts of inane little traditions around here. It's part of the charm, you see."

We came out of the hallway and into a large room full of comfortable chairs. Like the other room, its walls were lined with the heads of dead animals. Mostly deer, but some of them exotic animals—Cape buffalo, elands, a rhino, various African antelopes.

"As to the ground rules. As far as everybody here is aware, you are our newest member. As such, I must therefore tell you a little about the lodge. We were established in 1928 by Mrs. Warren Overcliff—that's *Judge* Overcliff? Of the law firm? And the various buildings and companies that bear his name to this day?"

I nodded vaguely.

"Now, Sunny, the Hellespont Lodge is distinguished by being the only all-female hunting lodge in the state of Georgia. But I might add that it is, nonetheless, among the most prestigious in the state. Our members are drawn exclusively from the upper stratum of Georgia society. As such there are certain proprieties we insist upon. Also certain *traditions.*" She smiled brightly and batted her eyes a few times. She reminded me all too much of my mother.

"With that in mind, it is *terribly* important that you comport yourself in a manner consistent with the spirit of the lodge. No one here but myself is aware that you are here 'on assignment,' as it were. Now I don't mean to seem rude, but I must be blunt and ask that you not engage in any . . . ah . . . *gratuitous* socializing here. Do your job, conduct yourself professionally, and when you have completed your work, file your report with me. Otherwise, I would ask that you conduct yourself as privately as possible, blend in—*as best you can*"—flap, flap, flap went the eyelashes—"and keep to yourself."

I had an urge to punch Mrs. Dale Herrington right in the middle of her pretty face. But I figured that wouldn't help me much in completing the assignment.

"So. Let me address the proprieties first. Members do not discuss business here. At one time, of course, that would not have been an issue, but these days you younger women insist upon having *careers.*" She made a brief sour face. "No matter, that's all to your own choosing, but what I mean is, we can't have members talking about in*vest*ments or handing around business cards or anything of that nature. We are here to enjoy the treasures of God's natural world, and to retreat from the pressures and intrigues and demands of the world. Nothing else.

"As to the *traditions.*" She spoke the word as many old-school Southern women do, reverently. "There are no firearms in the lodge. Our gamekeeper, Horst

Krens—or his assistant, Biggs—is available at all times to store, clean, and load your firearms. When you're ready to hunt, Horst or Biggs will retrieve your rifle from the gun room and escort you to any one of the forty or so permanent stands we maintain on the preserve."

"Actually," I said, "I'm a bow hunter."

One auburn eyebrow went up slightly. "Really?" She smiled and batted her eyelashes. It was obvious she put bowhunters in the same category as people who ran over road signs with their monster trucks. "Well. I suppose there's nothing wrong with that, is there? Other rules. No wearing of makeup is allowed. No carrying of purses. No stockings, no heels, no hairspray. With that little bitty figure of yours, this is no issue, but no girdles, either. This is a *woman's* realm here, and all things intended for the pursuit of the male species are strictly prohibited." She went on at some length with various other rules of a similarly silly nature.

"Actually," I said, cutting her off after she'd gone on for a while, "I've been acquainted with most of this."

The red eyebrow went up again. "By *whom*?"

"I thought you knew," I said. "My mother is a member of the lodge."

Suddenly her manner changed. It was a terribly subtle thing. Subtle and yet profound, if you know how to read the signs. "And that would be . . ."

"Miranda Wiseberg."

There was a brief batting of eyelids. "Oh, my. Here I've been treating you like some *hired* girl." Out came a small and very expensive-looking Motorola walkie-talkie from beneath her robe. Apparently the sacred traditions of the place didn't bar them from using frequency-hopping digital encryption radios. "Uma. Miss Childs and I are in the study. I need a pot of coffee, a chop medium-rare, and the usual sides. Greens, potatoes, string beans, whatever. I need a space heater. I need something warm. A hot water bottle, something like that. And I need it yesterday. Our new guest is hungry and she's cold."

I was neither. What I was, was bone tired. I just wanted to go to bed. But obviously that was no concern of Mrs. Dale Herrington IV's.

"So my *goodness*! A private investigator! Miranda Wiseberg's daughter is a private *eye*. That is so *exciting*." Suddenly she was batting her eyes and pursing her lips and pulling out chairs and fussing with my robe. From the impact of my revelation, it was clear that Mom was some sort of big wheel around this ridiculous place.

"Look," I said. "I appreciate the gesture and all, but it's late and I'm tired. I presume you brought me to this particular room for a reason."

"Well, yes, naturally . . ." The fussing and the lip pursing stopped. Martha Herrington's face went nervous. She turned and pointed at a place on the floor, just to the left of the rear door to the room. "There," she said.

I stood, picked up the candelabrum off the table, walked across the dark room. My footsteps echoed hollowly as I crossed the big slate flagstones. "Here?" I said. "Is this where Jennifer Treadaway was killed?"

Before she could answer, I heard something echoing down the hallway. A distant, bloodcurdling scream.

Mrs. Dale Herrington IV's comment, though not as ladylike as I might have expected from a woman of her station, was right on point:

"Oh *shit!*" she howled.

CHAPTER 3

I RAN BACK down the hallway in the direction from which the scream had seemed to come. At the end of the hall I found the bloodless woman. She was on her hands and knees, picking up pieces of broken china off the floor. It appeared she had fallen and dropped a pot of coffee.

Behind me Martha Herrington arrived out of breath. "Merciful heavens, Uma!" she said. "You scared the fool out of us. What in creation is wrong with you?"

The pale woman looked up from the floor but didn't speak.

At that moment I heard running footsteps and a middle-aged man appeared in the doorway. I took him to be the gamekeeper, Horst Krens. He was at least as pale and blond as the woman on the floor. Other than that, the main thing I noticed was the gun. As game-keeper, it was not surprising that, on hearing a scream, he had come running with a gun in his hand. But it was the *kind* of gun he carried that surprised me. If he'd come in with a shotgun or a rifle, it would hardly have surprised me under the circumstances. I'm not a gun nut, but in this line of work you need to be conversant with weaponry: I recognized the weapon the gamekeeper carried as an MP-5 submachine, the worldwide favorite of SWAT teams and gung-ho military units like the Navy SEALs.

"False alarm, Horst," Martha Herrington said. "Your sister is getting careless again. Sunny, let's go." She swept back down the hallway to the big room where Jennifer Treadaway had died.

When we reached the big room, Martha Herrington said, "I'm not heartless, but sometimes you have to be firm with the help. Horst is a marvel, but that sister of his . . . well, she's a *formidable* cook, but let's just say her skills end the moment she walks out the door of the kitchen. She's a *mute*, you know. Utterly incapable of speech." She put her hands together as though praying, then surveyed the room. "Now. Where were we?"

"Jennifer Treadaway."

"Of course, of course." She shook her head sadly. "I know it's late but this is *such* an unpleasant business, I just want to get it out of the way."

I nodded.

"It's the mystery of the thing. That's what's so terrible. We all got up, just like any ordinary day, and we came in here." She shuddered, maybe just a little theatrically. "And there she was."

"She'd been stabbed? Is that right?"

"Yes. In the neck. There was gore everywhere and . . . oh . . . it was simply sickening."

"Was the murder weapon ever found?"

"No."

"Do most of the women here carry hunting knives?"

"Well, when they're hunting, I suppose, yes. But this happened during the night. It's not like we go around with bush knives strapped to our nightgowns."

"What about the autopsy? Did it show what type of weapon was used?"

Martha Herrington waved her hand dismissively. "You'll need to talk to the sheriff about all that sort of thing. The *details*."

"But you suspect it was a member of the lodge who committed murder."

"Oh, my goodness no! I'm sure it was someone among the help."

"How big is the staff here?"

"I'll give you a list in the morning. It's fewer than ten people. Horst and Uma Krens. Plus Biggs. Plus a number of"—she lowered her voice slightly—"*colored* persons. Maids, groundskeepers, skinners, that sort of thing."

"And everybody working here now was working here then?"

"More or less, I think so."

I studied her face for a while. "Look," I said finally. "If you really suspected the staff, you would have brought me here undercover as a staff member. But you didn't. You brought me here in the guise of a new member. Which means you suspect it was a member of the lodge."

She flushed. "Well. There is that *possibility*."

"I'll need a complete membership list, and a complete list of who was staying at the lodge the night of the murder."

Martha Herrington pursed her lips. "I hope I've stressed clearly how important the notion of confidentiality is here. Under no circumstances is anyone to know that you've received such a list."

"At Peachtree Investigations, client confidentiality is an absolute," I said. "With one conspicuous exception. We will not conceal anything of a criminal nature. If I turn up anything implicating somebody of a crime, I don't care if it's a member or not, I pass it on to the cops. Period."

Martha Herrington looked at me without speaking.

"So tell me a little about the victim."

"Jennifer Treadaway, as I said, was Arvin Treadaway's wife. She was very active in the Atlanta community. Fund-raising, charity, so forth. I expect she's served on several of the same organizations as your mother. The Piedmont Hospital Ladies Auxiliary, Pediatric AIDS Foundation, the Margaret Mitchell House, things of that nature. Jennifer was a lovely woman. Gracious. Kind." She sniffed. "She's been greatly missed."

"Children?"

"Two. Arvin Junior is at Princeton and Bobby is still in high school. He goes to Westminster, of course."

"Hobbies?"

"She and Arvin were both avid sportsmen. They did grouse in Scotland, they did Argentina, they had a place in Idaho. And of course, Arvin's still got the plantation downstate, I think."

"Why do you say *still*?"

"Well, he was in a small financial bind for a brief period, but I don't think that lasted long."

"Any enemies? People she'd have a natural antipathy for?"

A big smile. "Why, honey, of *course* not."

"I just have one last question about this case," I said. "The cops investigated, they never found out anything.

Why open it up again? What's to be gained by bringing me in?"

Martha Herrington blinked. "Well, *obviously*. So it won't happen again."

I rubbed my eyes. "Look, I'm really fading. I'm afraid it's really time for me to get to bed."

Martha Herrington smiled suddenly. "Oh, sugar, I bet you are just *exhausted*. Let me show you your room."

We went through a maze of corridors and stairs, arriving finally at a room on the second floor.

"I have to ask you," I said as I opened the door to my room. "When Uma screamed earlier, Horst came running."

She cocked her head. "Yes . . ."

"Why was he carrying a submachine gun?"

"A *machine* gun!" Her eyebrows went up in surprise, and then she laughed gaily. "What a notion! A *machine* gun at the Hellespont Lodge!" Martha Herrington turned, walked briskly down the hallway, and disappeared.

CHAPTER 4

I AM NOT one of these happy, chatty, busy-little-humming-bird types in the morning. In the morning I want coffee and solitude. My best work is done at night. So when the banging on my door started circa four-thirty in the morning and the cheery voice started calling, "Up and at 'em, girls! Early bird gets the worm!"—let's just say the only thing that stopped me from getting out of bed and strangling someone was that I was so tired and wrecked and useless at that time of the morning that crawling out of bed was out of the question.

Soon I was asleep again.

But then at around 5 A.M. the banging and the annoyingly cheery voice started up again. And this time—not because I wanted to, or because I'm into self-abuse, but because I am a consummate freaking professional—I woke up and mumbled curses while pulling on my ludicrous camouflage outfit. (Yes, my friends: camouflage *shirt*, camouflage *jacket*, camouflage *pants,* camouflage *boots*, camouflage *gloves*, camouflage *baseball cap*. The only things that weren't camouflaged were my panties and my bra.)

The other ladies had all disappeared, presumably off to their hunting stands, by the time I'd taken my shower. Horst—he of the submachine gun—had apparently been waiting for me. "Let's go," he said in a curt, Teutonic accent. Then he didn't speak again as he led me out through the silent darkness, across a dark field of clover, through some woods, and then up into a hunting stand which stood a good twenty feet in the air and was built about as solidly as most people's houses. Horst disappeared on noiseless feet back into the gloom. The sun was just painting the horizon with a pale vermillion as I sat down to wait for whatever it was that hunters waited for at five o'clock in the morning. I propped my bow and my arrows against the wall of the stand and sat down in the folding chair which sat in the middle of the roofed stand.

Five o'clock in the morning and I sat there in the uncomfortable folding chair, clenching my fists. I don't know exactly what I was mad at, but I was mad, mad, mad, mad.

I remember mumbling, "Gee, I hope a deer comes so I can go down and strangle it with my bare hands."

And the next thing I knew, I was asleep.

Okay, so you're twenty pages or so into this book and you're going: *Is it me? Or is Sunny Childs one seriously short-tempered, foul-mouthed, annoying, opinionated, pissed-off chick?*

No, it's not you. It's me. It's totally me.

But before you get your panties in a wad and throw this book in the fire, let me assure you, I'm not always like this. It's just that I'd been going through a tense period with my boyfriend, which had culminated in a huge, knock-down drag-out fight the night before I came down to the lodge. It's just that I didn't want to do this assignment. It's just that I was going through one of those black stages which seem to infect my life about every two years. It's just that the whole world seemed to have gone dark on me, and I didn't know what to do about it.

And so when everything had started going wrong the night before, it had felt like the rain and the wreck and the weirdos in the woods and my freezing fingers had all arrived as the irrefutable and logical result of some movement of forces in my life over which I had no control. Under those circumstances some women cry. Me, I get mad.

Nuff said. I'll try to be nicer.

So let me back up and tell you a little about why I was so mad.

First, the assignment.

My boyfriend is a guy named Barrington Cherry. Please, no jokes about his name. Anyway, Barrington and I had planned a vacation for about six months. Barrington is in the FBI. And the FBI, believe me, is ground zero for the tight sphincter in America. Also ground zero for gratuitous paperwork. Also for "proper" procedure. Also for bureaucrat baloney. Which is to say that if you don't get your vacation approved months and months in advance, written down in triplicate, copies to all appropriate departments, signed by your supervisor, etc. etc. etc. in mind-numbing detail—well, forget about it.

So there we were. Tickets to Barbados paid for, hotel reservations made at some swank resort, scuba gear rented, FBI paperwork signed, mail to be held at the Post Office, paper delivery suspended. My name was even written in shocking pink on the big whiteboard calendar at Peachtree Investigations: SUNNY'S ON VACATION AND YOU CAN'T COME WITH HER! HAH HAH HAH! It was all settled. Barrington and I were having our first getaway in over a year. And we needed it. Like I say, things had been getting tense between us. For reasons I'll get into later.

So, three days before my vacation, Gunnar Brushwood walked into my office and said, "Sunny! Great news, kiddo. Got you a undercover assignment. You gonna love this."

"When?" I said, taking out my Palm Pilot.

"Next week."

Gunnar Brushwood is my boss, the owner of Peachtree Investigations. He is a big burly man's man with a deep Southern accent and a white handlebar mustache. He is a sweet man in his way. But not a good listener. When I told him I was on vacation next week, that an assignment at that time was an utter impossibility, he more or less ignored me, started talking about how Martha Herrington, the wife of Dale Herrington IV—you know, honey, the chairman of Herrington International?—needed an investigator, real big case, high-profile clients, tippy-top priority, blah blah blah blah blah. Gunnar will run on.

I tuned him out. When he was finally winded, I said, "Absolutely not. Can't do it."

Which is when he leaned forward and put the check in front of me. Fifty thousand bucks.

I don't consider myself to be a materialist. But that doesn't mean I can't be bought. Gunnar had started a profit-sharing arrangement with me, the result of which is that about fifteen thousand dollars of that check would go in my pocket. I started seeing home improvements, credit cards paid down, the possibility of retirement in something other than penury—you know, the usual.

All of which led to my bailing out of the vacation with Barrington. Let's just say the conversation didn't go well. Let's just say that Barrington went to Barbados and I didn't. Let's just put it there and leave it.

Gunnar, of course, left out the best part. The assignment would involve hunting. Yay! *Hunting!* Hunting? Me? Sunny Childs, the ultimate urbanaut, hanging out in the woods blasting away at deer? Screw that.

But there was that fifty-thousand-dollar check.

So instead of spending the next few days packing my sunscreen and trying on unflattering swimsuits, I was shooting my bow and arrow at a plastic deer and being taught the finer points of hunting lingo by Gunnar Brushwood, the great white hunter himself.

"Some pointy-head type fellow did a study one time, why people hunt," Gunnar was telling me as I drew my bow, released, missed the plastic deer for the umpeenth time. "What he determined, you got three types of hunters. Fifty percent of the people hunting in America are meat hunters. They're just poor folks looking to put some cheap protein on the family dinner table. Then you got trophy hunters. They comprise thirty percent of the total. Trophy hunters are driven by competitive urges. They want bigger antlers, longer spreads; they want exotic animal heads on the walls;

they want fancier weapons; they want trips to Africa. It's all about ego."

"That would be you," I said.

"In my weaker moments, maybe." Gunnar looked thoughtful for a moment. "Then you got what this fellow that did the study calls Spirit Hunters."

"Ooooo!" I said sarcastically. I released the arrow. I had been aiming at the eight-inch circle right behind the plastic deer's front shoulder. The arrow thunked into the plastic deer's head. "Crap."

"The reason you're missing is you're shooting from your head." He touched my stomach. "Shoot from here."

"Master say, he who shootee from belly, go velly welly into haht of Bambi."

Gunnar ignored me. "Spirit hunters are an interesting bunch. The demographic profile on them is, they're highly educated, many of them practice martial arts, they read a lot, often they're what you might call religious seekers. They view hunting as a spiritual journey, a means of connecting with the natural world."

"Oh," I said. "Like, shooting Bambi in the head is chicken soup for the soul?" I put another arrow in the bow, yanked the string back, released. It stuck in the ground between the plastic deer's feet. "Oopsy-daisy!"

Gunnar grabbed the bow out of my hands, threw it on the ground. I was surprised to see his face clouded with anger. He stared at me for a while.

"Sunny?" he said finally. "I been taking shit from you for a long time about hunting. I know, I know, I'm a pompous windbag sometimes and I tend to go on about my little enthusiasms at unnecessarily great length. I'm not unaware of that. But I want you to sit down and listen to me. What I'm going to say is not bullshit. It's not a joke. It's a real thing that comes from my heart, and so I would ask you to listen with at least a moderate show of respect. Not because it'll help you do this assignment better—which it will—but because your arrogance sometimes makes it impossible for you to see what's right in front of your face."

"Hey, whatever."

"No, not whatever. Sit down, shut up, listen." Gunnar had never, not once, talked to me this way before.

I sat sullenly, feeling like a little girl being scolded in school.

"I'm sorry about throwing your bow on the ground," he said. "That was wrong of me."

"Forget about it. It's just a stick and a string."

"No, it's not, Sunny. It's a great deal more than that." Gunnar looked over at the plastic deer for a while, then turned and pointed at the line of steel towers that poked up from the Atlanta skyline miles off in the distance. From where we stood, those great towers seemed fairly inconsequential. "Someday, all that stuff over there will crumble and fall away. It's in the nature of things."

He picked up my bow and hefted it in his hands.

"What will not disappear or crumble or decay," he went on, "is the human spirit. The human spirit arose from the soil. The human spirit came out of the trees and sifted down out of the air and grew up in the grasses on the African plains a million years ago. Right there in the middle of the lions and antelope and wildebeest and elephants. They were us and we were them. Just a bunch of beasts trying to make it. And you know something, Sunny? All of the air-

conditioned buildings, all the cell phones, all the Cadillacs with the On-Star System and the 12 DVD
changer in the trunk, all the 747s and computers and
intercontinental ballistic missiles will not change that.

"The human spirit contains within it both the desire
to destroy and dominate, and the desire to love and
join and create and build. You can't have one without
the other. People sit around in their little suburban
homes and they pretend that the human spirit only has
a bright side, that life's all Sunday brunch and ring-
around-the-rosy and furniture from the Pottery Barn.
They numb their desires with TV and booze and boring, bloodless churches and they pretend, pretend, pretend." His eyes seemed haunted for a moment. "But
it's sucking the air out of our lungs."

Gunnar bent the bow across his leg, restrung it,
flexed it, took aim at the plastic deer.

"When you go out into the woods to hunt," Gunnar
said, slowly letting the bow string down, "a force of
concentration is required which is unlike anything most
people are able to muster in their day-to-day life. You
know what it starts with? Silence. You sit there, Sunny,
and you sit there and you sit there. Silent as death.
Waiting for a sign. And soon you begin to hear bugs
walking in the grass, the wind stirring a branch in a
tree so far away you can't see it. A click, a stick breaking, an exhaled breath, a smell—you have to tune into
all of that. Because that's what's going to tell you that
your quarry is about to come into range. This is not
something you can explain."

"Why not just go out there and take pictures?" I said.
"Why do you have to *kill*?"

"Because pictures don't get at the heart of the thing."

"And that would be what?"

"All I can say is go out there into the woods and release yourself. Release yourself utterly to what you feel and I guarantee you this, Sunny, you will never be the same."

"I don't know what you're talking about."

"This," he said. "We all have *this*." He smiled thinly as he released the arrow. It stuck into the plastic deer right behind the shoulder.

"I don't get it."

"The killer instinct."

"No," I said. "*I* don't."

"Keep kidding yourself, Sunny."

"It's all a big macho guy thing."

Gunnar laughed like he knew something I didn't.

When I woke up in my stand in the trees, I felt somewhat restored. It was a beautiful Indian summer day. The storms of the night before had disappeared, leaving the woods pleasant and green. Autumn comes later than hunting season in Georgia.

I yawned and stretched, leaned out over the edge of the stand, and looked at the carpet of pine needles on the ground. To my right was a stretch of pine trees. In front of me lay a small creek surrounded by scrubby hardwoods and briars. To my left was a field of clover. Around me I could hear the soft rustle of wind. Otherwise the world seemed utterly silent. After about ten minutes I was bored stiff. I stood up and did some calisthenics, looked at my watch. It was five minutes 'til nine o'clock.

Gunnar had assured me that if I wanted to appear as though I was even vaguely serious about hunting, I needed to stay in the stand until ten o'clock. I made a mental note to sneak my laptop up in my backpack tomorrow. Maybe I could catch up on paperwork.

Another ten minutes and I began getting irritable. How could people stand this? There wasn't anything moving out there. Not a bird, not a squirrel, not a butterfly. And there were most certainly no deer. I started going over all my little wounds, thinking about my fight with Barrington, about the three days of abuse I'd suffered from Gunnar as I shot my bow at his plastic deer, thinking about the way Martha Herrington had treated me the night before until suddenly my connection to Mother was revealed.

"This," I said loudly, "is most surely the dumbest thing in the entire world." I wasn't sure if I was talking about the case, about hunting, or about my life.

As usual, I was wrong on all counts. Things were about to become very interesting.

CHAPTER 5

WHEN I GOT back to the lodge, lunch was being served in a sort of café in the back. I looked into the room, saw all these attractive rich women sitting around in their expensive hunting outfits, and got a sinking feeling in my gut. There were about thirty or so of them, and without spending more than five seconds looking at them, I had a sudden flashback to my experience in high school. My mother had come from a fairly humble background, married well on her second stab at the marriage game, and suddenly we were flush. With the result that I was dumped into a fancy private school on the north side of Atlanta at age fourteen, feeling like some kind of alien. In high school all the girls were beautiful and bosomy and sophisticated and knew how to dress. And then there was me: none of the above.

So instead of taking lunch, I decided to go down to the sheriff's office and dig up the case file on Jennifer Treadaway's murder.

The county seat of Williams County, Georgia, was a wide spot in the road called Hightower. It is nearly impossible to describe just exactly what a broken-down, benighted, pitiful wreck of a town it was.

Downtown Hightower consisted of ten boarded-up stores, a pawn shop, a video arcade, a barber shop, a feed store, and a courthouse whose red sandstone outlines had obviously been ornately and proudly carved at great expense some great many years ago, but the details had all blurred and run and worn away beneath the rain and wind until the place looked like a red lump, a huge anthill ready to be idly stomped into the ground by the passing of some indolent giant.

A sign on the door of the dim, high-ceilinged second floor said, TEDDY T. TIMMERS, SHERIFF.

I entered, found a large, nearly empty room in the middle of which sat a fat black man with his feet on a desk, eating a hamburger. Ketchup had dripped from the burger onto a white trash bag which he had tucked like a bib into the neck of his brown uniform. He looked at me as though astonished.

"Sheriff Timmers?"

The look of astonishment lasted four or five more seconds. "Oh. No, ma'am. He in the back." He gestured with the hamburger at a large door covered with peeling brown paint.

"My name is Sunny Childs. I was told he would be expecting me sometime today."

He set the hamburger down. "*Expecting* you? The sheyuff?"

"Yes. The sheriff. Timmers. He's expecting me."

The fat deputy frowned. "Huh. I be dawg." He stood, walked through the door. A virtually encyclopedic collection of law enforcement paraphernalia hung from his belt, clattering as he moved: cuffs, walkie-talkie, ancient revolver, baton, pepper spray, speed-loaders, shotgun shells, a hunting knife, and a few other things I didn't have time to make out. He was ready for bear.

A large fly buzzed slowly across the room, landed on the wall next to me. After a moment or two it fell off the wall and lay there on its back, feet struggling feebly.

I watched until it stopped moving. Finally the fat deputy came back out. "Sheyuff be wif you in a minute, ma'am. Just make yourself at home." He put the garbage bag bib back on and tucked into his hamburger, smacking his lips and grunting appreciatively from time to time.

After a few minutes, a very tall black woman in a nurse's uniform came out. "I'm Rochelle Longineau," she said, extending her hand. "Sheriff Timmers's nurse." I shook her hand, which was large and firm. Each of her fingers was tipped with a long, curved, blood red nail.

"Nurse?" I said.

She smiled, showing me a wide row of white teeth. "Bless his heart, Sheriff Timmers is in somewhat poor health at this moment." I followed her down a short hallway, past an empty secretarial desk and into a large high-ceilinged office. The room must have been eighty-five degrees.

"I apologize for the heat, Miss Childers." The voice came out of a huddled lump heaped in the chair behind the desk.

"It's Childs," I said. "Sunny Childs."

Two small blue eyes peered at me out of a mass of

wrinkles. "Don't got no circulation in my . . ." The blue eyes seemed to lose focus for a moment.

"Extremities," the nurse said.

"Extremities. I forget words. Since the stroke." A thin green streak of drool ran out of the wrinkled crevasse which must have been his mouth. A blue-veined hand fluttered on the desk, struggled briefly into the air, then settled back down onto the wood. "That's why-come I got to have the heat in here."

The nurse pulled out a chair for me and then went around to the other side of the desk, where she began feeding him strained peas out of a baby food jar.

I sat. "I appreciate your seeing me today. I believe Mrs. Herrington called to alert you that I would be looking into the Jennifer Treadaway case on behalf of the Hellespont Lodge."

The little blue eyes gleamed. "You just a little bitty thang, ain't you, doll. What you weigh? Ninety-seven? Ninety-eight?"

"Don't mind him," the nurse said. "The stroke has affected his impulse control. Makes him say inappropriate things sometimes. It's purely a medical condition and I assure you he means nothing by it."

"I been high sheriff down here since nineteen and fifty-six. Reckon I'll be the last white man to ever serve here." The old man made a wheezing laugh, spitting strained peas onto the desk. "Gone be wall-to-wall coons around this place once the Lord takes me."

"Like I say," the nurse said dryly.

"Yes, Sheriff. As I was saying about the case? Jennifer Treadaway?"

The little blue eyes stared out of the wrinkles. "Who?"

"The dead lady," the nurse said.

"The dead lady. The dead lady." The wrinkles deepened. "What, somebody died?"

"Remember? Last year? At the lodge."

The light came on in the little blue eyes. "Oh, yeah. Tragic thing. The dearly departed will be sorely missed, Praise the Lord, blah blah blah." The sheriff rolled his eyes, made a fugitive but humorous gesture with a couple of fingers.

"So, what I'm looking for is a briefing on your investigation, Sheriff."

The sheriff made some labial sounds, working on his strained peas. "A briefing," he said finally. He frowned. "What it was, one of these rich ladies over to the hunting lodge got herself cut. Slit like a hog. Praise the Lord and pass the biscuits. Hope I'm not shocking you, missy."

"No, sir, this is my job."

"Bet you good in the sack, huh?" One blue eye disappeared briefly. "Hot tamale, huh? *Mui picante, no?*"

"Sheriff? You don't mind if we stick to the subject?"

The wrinkles moved up and down. "Treadaway. That was the lady's name, if I recollect. Got herself cut. Slit like a hog. Never did figger out who done it."

I looked at the nurse. "Help me out here. Is there somebody a little more *compos mentis* here? Maybe the investigating officer?"

"Address your questions to me, young lady," the sheriff said.

"He *is* the investigating officer, Miss Childs," the nurse said. Her face was an impassive mask.

"You went out there yourself?" I said. "Did the crime scene, the whole bit?"

"My colored girl here, she tuck me out in my wheelie chair," the sheriff said. "Naturally we had some assistance from the state police. Legwork type of thing."

"I see," I said.

"The sheriff was noted for his investigative abilities," the nurse said. "Back before the stroke."

"And when was the stroke?" I said.

"Nineteen eighty-three."

"You have great comic timing," I said.

Her face remained impassive.

"Tell Deputy Coon out there to get me the file on Treadaway," he said.

"Is that really his name?" I said.

The nurse gave me a look like: *Now, who's being funny?* Then she stood up and walked out of the room. I sat in silence for a while, my clothes beginning to stick to my body from the heat while the old man sat slumped over in his wheelchair.

Eventually the sheriff looked up and said, "You mind feeding me some peas? I'm getting a powerful hankering."

Before I had a chance to decide how I wanted to handle the feeding issue, the nurse came back with a thin file folder, which she handed to the sheriff. One ancient, gnarled hand closed around the cardboard, then a second hand crept out from inside the robe he was wearing and arduously opened the folder. A single sheet of paper slid out of the folder and drifted lazily to the floor.

The blue eyes stared at the empty folder and a sort of bleak silence enveloped the room.

"Let me get that," I said, stooping to pick up the piece of paper.

It was a single mimeographed page, printed in bleary purple ink. I don't think I've seen an actual mimeographed piece of paper since elementary school. At the top it said UNIFORM CRIME REPORT.

Underneath, the form listed the name of the victim and a few minor particulars of the crime. There was no mention of a suspect, no reference to witness reports or an autopsy, no crime scene photos. In short, there was nothing here at all.

I looked at the bright little blue eyes, then at the impassive gaze of Nurse Longineau.

"Has there been any investigation at all?" I said.

"Something I noticed, Nurse," he said. "Lot of the gals I liked best in the sack, I couldn't tolerate as soon as they opened their mouths. Some kind of joke God played on the male species, I do believe. Praise the Lord and pass the ammunition!" He let out a groaning cackle.

"Maybe I should see you out," the nurse said.

We walked back down the corridor and out into the entry room of the Williams County Sheriff's Department. The fat deputy was gone, but there was a large ketchup stain in the middle of the empty floor to show he'd been there.

"Welcome to Williams County," Rochelle Longineau said.

"That's *it*?" I said. "One piece of paper? That's his whole investigation?"

"Look, Miss Childs, here it is: not much goes on in this county of a criminal nature. Actually not much goes on here, period. We only have eight thousand citizens in the entire county. So the occasional fist fight is about it. In the rare cases that something bad happens, we call the GBI, they handle everything."

"You have a name?"

"Sure, come on over to my office." She indicated a door across the hallway. I stepped inside, found myself in a room with carpet on the floor, cut flowers in a vase on a modern desk, air-conditioning, a new computer. It was as though I'd walked out of the nineteenth century and into—if not the twenty-first century, then at least the twentieth. I had a strange feeling looking at it, like I was on the verge of some kind of understanding.

Rochelle Longineau smiled for a fraction of a second. "You were wondering why I would demean myself by working for that man," she said.

"It had crossed my mind."

"When he dies, I intend to be sheriff."

"You're a nurse."

"You think Sheriff Timmers is a trained law enforcement expert?" Another mirthless smile. She sat, tapped some keys on the computer. The laser printer next to her desk began to whine and spit out paper. "I'm developing a sort of shadow operation here. Soon as I get elected, all the old clowns like the deputy you met earlier will have to go."

The printer stopped printing.

"Meantime, fiscal realities in a county like this are such that professional investigatory skills are prohibitively expensive. For an investigation of a serious crime, we rely now, and will rely in the future, on the state." She pulled the papers out of the printer and said,

"Here are my records of the investigation—such as it is—of the murder of Jennifer Treadaway."

I glanced through what she had. It wasn't much, but it was something. A list of witnesses, an inventory of items taken from the crime scene, and a summary of the disposition of the case. The last page simply said, "Case referred to Georgia Bureau of Investigation."

"You'll want to talk to Agent Allgood over at the GBI," she said. "He's an efficient investigator and he did what he could with this case."

My brow furrowed. "That sounds a little cryptic. What do you mean, he did what he could?"

The nurse scratched her head delicately with one long red fingernail. "I'm not quite sure how to put this," Rochelle Longineau said. "But I think you'd do well to drive back to Atlanta and forget all about this thing."

I kept looking at her, puzzled.

"Those women over there," Longineau said, "they're bad people. That lodge is a bad place. Everybody around here knows it."

"Okay, hold on, now you're sounding like somebody out of a vampire movie."

Longineau sighed. "See, I'm having trouble explaining myself. So let me give you a little history on this place. Williams County was at one time the richest county in Georgia. You believe that? The plantations here were large, well managed, and extremely profitable. This would have been, say, the 1850s. But then you had the war, and then after that, maybe in the 1870s or '80s, cotton prices dropped and the soil wore out. Things around here went bad fast. All the rich white folks, the plantation owners, they just up and moved on. Found better soil or other pursuits. And the overseers, they headed west. The crackers, they drifted on upstate or off to Alabama. And the plantations? They just melted away like sugar in the rain. The forests just took 'em back. And precious little was left around here but the ancestors of the many, many slaves who'd worked this wretched dirt a very long time ago."

The nurse—or shadow sheriff or whatever she was— leaned back in her nice leather chair. "The biggest landowner in Williams County is now Georgia Pacific, the lumber people. Second is Weyerhauser. Third is National Pulp and Paper. Fourth is the Hellespont Lodge. You have to go all the way down to number three-twelve on the tax rolls before you find a property owner who actually lives within the confines of Williams County. What I'm getting at is this: that bunch of pretty white ladies over there at that hunting lodge can buy and sell every soul in this county."

"I'm still not following you."

"Please. I'm doing my best." She held up her hand. "What I'm saying is that those ladies over there are a law unto themselves. Untouchable. The plain-out truth is, Williams County could no more investigate a criminal matter over at the Hellespont Lodge than we could send a man to the moon." She paused. "Not if they didn't want us to, anyway."

"Are you suggesting they didn't want this matter investigated?"

"Here's what I'm saying. I'm no detective. But I'm no simpleton either. So it was entirely clear to me that by the time we got there, evidence had been tampered with, the crime scene had been sanitized, the body very possibly moved . . ." She shook her head. "It was a joke."

"Yeah, but didn't you say the GBI did the investigation? They're a pretty professional outfit."

"Look. I'm not saying the Georgia Bureau of Investigation is a corrupt organization. Far from it. But they get over there, the crime scene is not fruitful, the ladies tell some cockamamie story about what happened. And then the lawyers from Atlanta start showing up." She shrugged. "I don't profess to be some great political sophisticate, but I read the papers. I get up to Atlanta now and again. I make a point to keep informed. And those men who showed up, those lawyers, they were people you see in the papers. Not junior partners, not associates. I'm talking about top dogs. The five-hundred-dollar-an-hour boys."

"Let me ask you a question, then," I said. "I've been hired by the leadership of the Hellespont Lodge to investigate this crime. If they were really trying to cover up what happened, why would they hire me?"

"That's the question, isn't it?"

I picked up the papers, put them in my briefcase.

"This is not the first time this happened, you know," Rochelle Longineau said. "There have been several, shall we say, 'accidents' over the years. In fact, the lodge was established after the owner was shot. Everybody knew he got shot by his wife."

"Everybody who?"

Rochelle gave me a funny look. "Black folks, back in the day, we had eyes but we were nonpersons. You see what I mean?"

"You're saying somebody who worked there saw the crime?"

"Sure. Six or seven people, in fact. Nineteen twenty-six, Granada Woodward was down there quail hunting with her husband, Ernest. Standing right in front of the hack driver and the dog boy and the gun bearers and the valets, she shot him smack through the head."

"Well, it could have been an accident."

This drew a rich, long laugh. "Even colored folks know you don't hunt quail with double ought buckshot. Blew his head clean off. A retarded black man was duly imprisoned for the crime, six black people—witnesses, quote unquote—received two thousand dollars cash, and Granada Woodward got six point three million dollars, a mansion in Buckhead, and a ten-thousand-acre plantation. Which she later set up as Hellespont Lodge."

"And you know this how?"

"My grandfather was Ernest Woodward's dog boy. Two thousand dollars was an enormous sum in 1926. My grandfather put his money to use, rather shrewdly, given the limitations of his time and place. Before he sent me off to the University of Georgia, he sat me down and explained to me why I was not permitted to squander what I was being given. The price of my education, he said, was a liability made good in blood and lies. It was up to me, he said, to pay down that debt."

"Wow."

"I said it before, I'll say it again. That place is no good. You seem like an earnest, hardworking lady trying to do a good job. I was you? I'd send my check back to the ladies and get the heck out of Dodge."

CHAPTER 6

THE NEAREST POST of the Georgia Bureau of Investigation was up in Macon, an hour's drive from Williams County. It was a low building built of dun-colored brick situated on a cheap piece of land near a commercial strip just off the bypass. I asked for Agent Allgood, then sat down in a hard chair and waited for at least an hour.

Finally a short stocky man wearing a blue cotton shirt, cowboy boots, and khakis came out. He had thinning hair, a tobacco plug in one cheek, and a sour expression on his face.

"Miss Childs?"

I jumped up and put out my hand. "How are you, Agent Allgood."

He looked at my hand like it had been dipped in sewage. "You're wasting your time," he said.

"Excuse me?"

"I said, don't let the doorknob hit you in the keister on the way out."

"Hold on, hold on," I said. "Where's this coming from?"

Agent Allgood whispered something to the uniformed receptionist, then walked away without answering.

I had left my cell back at the lodge, so I had to ask the receptionist if I could bum her phone for a moment.

Without looking up from her computer she said, "Pay phone's down at Arby's."

I called the Hellespont Lodge from Arby's, told Martha Herrington I'd hit a snag trying to get information out of the GBI.

"Is it that little Allgood person?" she said.

"Right."

"We'll fix his wagon. I'll make some calls. By the time you get back there, he'll be asking if he can wash your car."

He wasn't quite that eager to please, but whoever Martha Herrington had called had gotten some results: a very chastened-looking Agent Wayne Allgood was waiting for me on the curb with a cup of coffee when I drove up in my mother's Jag.

"Hit a deer or something?" he said, surveying the damage to the front of the car.

"Or something," I said.

"Well." He handed me the cup of coffee, spit some tobacco juice on the thin grass, then said in a resigned voice, "Come on in, I guess."

I followed him back to a small, bare office. "Look, Miss Childs," he said as we sat down. "I ain't apologizing for my behavior. Department policy is, we don't release nothing to PIs."

"That's no excuse for being rude."

He eyed me for a while. "I won't lie to you. This case was a cover-up from day one. That bunch of rich old ladies over there interfered with this investigation every step of the way. And now suddenly they're sending a PI over here, acting like we was a bunch of incompetents and they need to send somebody over to clean up after me? Huh-uh. I ain't gonna apologize, not a lick."

"I don't know anything about that," I said. "All I know is I've been hired to do a job."

"Well, lotsa luck, sweetheart."

"So I gather somebody called you from on high and said you could share your files with me."

Agent Allgood took a Dixie cup out of the drawer of his desk, spit some tobacco juice in it, then put it back in the drawer. "I am entirely at your disposal," he said, his voice flat and uninflected.

"Great. Tell me about the murder of Jennifer Treadaway."

He reached behind him, took a fat folder off the credenza, and tossed it on the desk. "It's all there. For whatever it's worth. By the time I showed up, she'd been lying there for a good eight, ten hours. Maybe more. They found the body at four in the morning and I didn't get a call from Williams County till noon. Took me an hour and a half to get there.

"By that time the maids had cleaned up all the blood. The body had been covered with a wool blanket that had dog hair and God knows what-all on it, thereby contaminating all fiber evidence. Every lady in the lodge had tromped through the room. And that's only the crime scene itself. The worst thing, there were at least ten lawyers in the building. Good lawyers, too. I wanted to interview anybody, I had to go through a lawyer. I wanted to search people's rooms or anything of that nature, there was some son of a bitch standing in front of the door in a two-thousand-dollar suit, smiling at me and asking what my probable cause was to walk through that door. Took me three weeks just to lay hands on a membership list for the lodge."

"Okay, but what *did* you find?"

He opened the file, handed me some pictures. They showed a very pretty woman lying on the floor on her back, her hands crossed over her chest. The right side of her face was bright red.

"You can see the lividity on the side of the face. She'd obviously been lying on her side for a long period of time. But somebody had moved her. Nobody would admit to doing it, but it must have been one of the maids. There was slight rigor mortis in the extremities. Her body temp was in the low eighties. She was wearing a nightgown. Knife blade entered her neck from the left side, went through the carotid and up into the brain stem."

I nodded. It always gave me a strange feeling looking at pictures like this. Some people find them nauseating, but they always affected me differently; it was more like I felt embarrassed, as though I were invading some private moment.

"You never found a murder weapon."

"Not so far as we know. ME believed it was an extremely sharp knife with a four-to five-inch blade, consistent with a hunting knife. I have no doubt that every woman in the lodge had a hunting knife on her hip the day before the crime—but by the time I got past the lawyers, there wasn't a knife on the property."

"Did you luminol the room?"

He nodded. "Obviously you know that luminol

makes it so you can reveal very small quantities of blood under ultraviolet light. I sprayed the walls and floor with luminol and the results are that I was able to find a goodly-sized blood splotch on the wall by the fireplace." He passed me a ghostly photograph, a splotch of purple light on the wall. "As you can see, the margins of the blood are all smeared from when it got washed off. So there's no way of doing blood spatter analysis on it. For all I know, some gal had come in there after cleaning a deer and wiped her hand on the wall."

"You swabbed for DNA?"

"Sure. Tried anyway. But they'd cleaned the place very thoroughly. With bleach. The quantities of blood left on the wall were minute, and bleach breaks down the amino acids anyway, so DNA results were useless."

"Prints?"

"I fumed the room with cyanoacrylate. You want to hear something fascinating? Other than a couple of prints from the maids, there was not one single latent print in that entire room."

"No kidding. So the maid was pretty thorough."

"My experience, maids are like everybody else on the planet. They don't volunteer to do work they don't have to. Somebody *instructed* that maid to clean the living daylights out of that room. Every wall, every flagstone, every chair, every table, every lamp . . ."

"My God," I said.

"Not only that. The maid had washed the victim's *feet*. Now why would somebody wash a dead person's feet?" He tossed me a picture of two bare white feet. "I could smell the bleach on them."

"I assume you raised hell?"

"Sure. But to what end? These rich ladies all just batted their eyes at me and gave me this routine about how, 'Oh, little old me, I didn't know we weren't supposed to clean up.' And when that didn't wash, they changed their story and said the sheriff told them they could do it."

"Which he confirmed?"

"You met that old goat. He's already got one foot in the grave."

"What about interviews?"

"The reports are in there. They're all the same." He spoke in a high, mincing tone. "Oh, she was such a *darling* woman, we loved her to *death*, and we are just ever so *devastated* and *shocked* and *saddened* at this terrible *tragedy*." He went back to his normal voice. "Otherwise? Didn't see nothing, hear nothing, or know nothing."

"And the maids?"

"Actually it was just one maid. I swear to God, that girl was dumb as a box of hair. I couldn't get a straight story out of her. Best I can recall, it was that gamekeeper who told her to clean up. I forget his name. Nazi-looking sumbitch."

"Horst Krens."

"That's the one. First, he denied that he told her to clean up. Then he says, he *thinks* maybe possibly probably conceivably—if he *did* by some off chance tell the maid to clean up—what it was, one of the ladies told him the sheriff had told her it was okay. Real vague, you know. Couldn't remember which lady, couldn't remember anything with a great deal of specificity."

"I still don't understand why you couldn't search for weapons."

Agent Allgood ground his teeth for a moment. "Like

I say, the lawyers had showed up by then. Asking for warrants and subpoenas and all this stuff. Now, an investigator has total access to a crime scene. That's common law, going back a million years. Problem is, it's a gray area how far out an investigator gets to say that the crime scene goes. Does it end at the edge of the room? The end of the hall? The perimeter of the building? You push the perimeter too far, a judge can throw out whatever you found, say it was an illegal search. Gets complicated. So I call my bosses, call the DA, so on, to get clearance how far I can search." Agent Allgood scowled. "It rapidly became clear to me that strings were being pulled, forces put in motion, you know what I mean? Everybody told me, the crime scene stops at the end of the hallways. No searching private rooms without PC."

"Without probable cause."

"Right. So naturally by the end of the day, all these gals have packed up their things in their Range Rovers and hit the road."

"What about the gun room? Anything in there?"

"Locked. Or so everybody said."

"And you weren't allowed to search it?"

Agent Allgood laughed without humor. "Now you see why I was so rude to you earlier? This whole case, I was set up to fail."

"How hard did you push?"

"Hard as I could." He rocked back and forth for a moment, his eyes focused on something in the distance. There was defeat in his shoulders. "Which is when I start hearing, for the first time in my career, whispers from the bosses about my lack of competence, various subtle indications that maybe I was hurting my career with this thing, make it easy on yourself, nobody likes to make waves when rich people are involved in un-solvable whodunnits, so on, so forth."

"You were basically told to tank the investigation."

"Oh my goodness, no! Not in so many words." He shook his head angrily. "It was all handled much more subtle than that." He took out his Dixie cup, spit the plug of tobacco into it. "Worst thing about it, them ladies over at that lodge, it's like they specialize in making you feel small. Oh, but it's all delicate as hell. Never come out and say what they mean. But you know. By God, you walk away from them people and you know you been whooped on. Whooped on bad, too. Had my druthers, I'd just as soon get beat with a stick as have a so-called polite conversation with one of them ladies."

"So what do you think really happened?"

"This is totally a guess. But I think she was walking barefoot outside somewhere around two o'clock in the morning. I think she ran into something she wasn't supposed to. And then she got killed. Whatever it was she wasn't supposed to see, the folks who killed her didn't want her there, so they dragged her inside the house, washed her feet to get off the dirt and leaves and whatever other evidence might be on them, then splashed some blood on the wall. Or maybe the blood ain't even connected."

"Who do you think did it?"

"I don't even have the first clue. I will say this: it was real clean. You wanted to kill somebody quick, you couldn't pick a better place. It went in once, it didn't come out. That suggests somebody who knew what they was doing. It wasn't anger, and it sure wasn't no accident."

"An employee?"

"Most of the people there haven't graduated elementary school. We're not talking about criminal geniuses. Whoever thought to wash her feet, my bet, they knew something about forensics."

"What about this Horst guy? What's his deal?"

"There was nothing in the crime computer on him. Clean credit rating. No wants or warrants, no judgments. He's here on a green card. German citizen. He was a gamekeeper on some preserve run for the commie bigwigs back in East Germany. Supposedly."

"Why do you say 'supposedly'?"

Agent Allgood squinted at me thoughtfully. "You've seen him. What's your first impression of him?"

"Ex-military."

Allgood nodded. "Yup. That's what I thought, too. Don't strike me he spent his whole career carrying shotguns for old fat guys."

"What about Biggs, Horst's assistant?"

Allgood's face seemed strangely blank. "I think he had an alibi."

"Why the funny face when I mention Biggs?"

"If I made a funny face, I didn't mean to. Far as Biggs goes, I wouldn't look at him too close."

"So . . . any conclusions at all? Likely suspects?"

"I truly, truly, truly wouldn't want to venture." He looked at me expressionlessly. "I made some calls before you got here, Sunny. You got a good reputation. Don't let these ladies ruin it."

"Why would they do that?"

He slid the file across the desk. "I don't know why them ladies hired you. But I bet you five dollars it ain't because they want this case solved. You be careful."

CHAPTER 7

GOT BACK to the lodge late in the afternoon. Gunnar had impressed upon me the importance of appearing gung-ho about hunting, so I dutifully pulled on my camo gear, consulted with Horst about a suitable tree stand—given the wind direction, time of day, phase of the moon, whatever—and then lugged my bow out to the hunting stand he recommended.

I looked at my watch after I'd climbed up the ladder and settled into the chair. It was just past four-thirty. The stand gave me a view of a brushy little draw with a small creek meandering through it and another field of clover. I leaned my elbows on the two by four in front of me, propped my chin on my hands, and stared out at the field. Dullsville. Just as had happened that morning, nothing moved. No crickets, no robins, no hawks, no squirrels, no lions, no zebras. No deer.

And once again, I fell dead asleep.

I woke to the sound of gunfire, a single loud slap that echoed once then died. Gunfire has a way of rousing you, and I woke in an instant, my heart racing. When I realized that it was almost certainly one of the ladies off in the woods blasting at some poor animal, my heart slowed and I looked out of the stand.

I was a little surprised to see four deer below me, three does and a fawn nearing adulthood. Their heads were high, ears pricked, and all four were peering intently in the direction of the gunshot. Apparently they hadn't noticed me.

I had never been this close to a deer before. They were lovely delicate animals, but somehow rounder in the body, more goat-like than I had expected. The deer were so close that I could see a tick lodged in the fur of one doe's shoulder, and a patchy skin disease on a hock of the fawn. They had the twitchy alertness of neurotic teenaged girls.

After a moment the deer apparently decided that the gunshot offered no immediate threat to their safety, so they began browsing, moving slowly away from me. I didn't want to spook them, so I tried not to move. I barely even breathed.

The deer continued to meander away. Having nothing else to do, I just watched them. After a while a young buck appeared, a strip of velvet hanging like a flag of surrender off the end of his thin new four-point antlers. He pawed the ground, snorted, then ambled out and began eating clover.

I don't know how long I watched, but there was something addicting about the feeling of sitting completely motionless, studying their behavior, and nursing the feeling that the animals I watched were completely unaware of my presence. Maybe Gunnar was right. Maybe we were losing something back there in the cities. I felt like I could see, hear, smell, feel more intently. But I didn't have the slightest urge to shoot anything.

Eventually the light started to fail. Just about the time that the sun had slipped down into the trees, I started getting antsy, ready to get back to the lodge and get to work. Suddenly, out of the corner of my eye, I saw a subtle movement back in the brushy creekbed. I turned my eyes, careful not to move my body, studied the brush. What was it I'd seen?

I must have kept my eyes glued to the brush for five minutes. Then I saw it again. Another subtle movement.

And suddenly it was as though it had materialized out of thin air: right where I'd been looking, right where only seconds earlier there had been nothing but a tangle of briars, there stood a strange and magnificent buck. It took me a moment to make out why he seemed so strange. First, he must have been nearly twice the bulk of the does out in the field, and his antlers were a massive spread of tines. But there was something about this huge buck's antlers that was different. In the failing light, I couldn't quite make out what it was.

But that wasn't the main thing that made this deer so strange. Even in the fading light I realized why he looked so odd. Except for a blob of gray on his throat, the buck's coat was entirely white.

For a moment my breath caught. The deer didn't move again for several minutes. I stared at him until my vision seemed to turn into a gray tunnel between me and him. Then, slowly, he began to move.

As he grew closer, I began to make out why his antlers had seemed so strange when I first saw them. In the books, you usually see deer with broad symmetrical antlers. But this buck wore an odd forest of tines and beams and bumps and ridges. I tried to count the number of points. Gunnar had schooled me that this was important to trophy hunters. According to him, in the South, a buck with eight points was considered to be very unusual. Ten was exceptionally rare. When I reached fifteen points, I lost track, started over, lost track, and gave up.

At that moment, a shot rang out and the smaller buck in the middle of the clover staggered, ran a few steps, then fell over. The other deer all bounded away with a vigorous, almost violent grace, the white flags of their tails disappearing into the dark woods inside of two seconds.

And the strange white buck? It was just gone. I didn't see it move, didn't hear it go. One second it was there, the next it wasn't.

For a moment I felt as our ancient forebears must have felt: as though I had been subject to some powerful magic. I tried to stand, but my legs wouldn't lift me, and for reasons I couldn't begin to fathom, I began to weep.

CHAPTER 8

FELT A worm of dread turning in my gut as I walked through the darkness toward the lodge. It was as though a switch had gone off in my brain, and suddenly the dark woods were my friend, and the lodge—and the people inside—had become the enemy. In the gloom behind the lodge I saw four deer hanging from chains. By the light of a flickering kerosene lamp I could barely make out Biggs, the gamekeeper's assistant, who was flaying the skin off one of them with a small, glinting little curve of steel.

And when I reached the lodge, it was every bit as bad as I'd expected. There they were, gathered in the very room where Jennifer Treadaway had been murdered: a whole room of pretty women, laughing brightly, showing off their expensive dental work as they sipped bourbon from their heavy vessels of cut glass. High school all over again. All those many years of breeding, all that charm and pretense, all that schooling, all that money, all that security in their hermetic little world of privilege and prosperity. I wanted to turn and flee back into the woods.

But this was where my work was.

As I entered the big room—its stone walls lined with the heads of dead deer and wild hogs and various other animals—Martha Herrington detached herself from the crowd. "Honey!" she howled. "I have been *looking* for youuuu!"

She grabbed me by the arm and introduced me to a knot of women. "Sunny Childs, I'd like you to meet the girls. Sunny Childs, Mrs. Rodney Childs, this is Bonnie Hathaway, Mrs. Tommy Hathaway; Elise Shore, Mrs. Walter Shore; Robin Vandecourt, Mrs. James Vandecourt, Jr.; Rose Ellen Knight, Mrs. Jimmy Dale Knight."

They were one more like the other. Thin, lovely, wide-eyed, fifty-ish trying to cling to thirty-nine-ish. Their laughter tinkled, kiss-kiss in the air, it's so *lovely* to meet you, you are going to have *such* a wonderful *time* at the lodge. It was just one more reminder of why—after suffering through four years with people like this in high school—I'd rushed up North to go to college.

After some dull patter, I detached myself from the group. "Um, Martha," I said. "What's this about me being *Mrs*. Rodney Childs? There is no Rodney Childs."

She looked at me with a peculiar expression. "Last night you said your mother had explained."

"Explained what?"

"Well, Sunny, this is a *married* women's club. You could hardly be a member without a husband."

"Oh."

"You'll need to come up with a story about Rodney. Obviously he must be wealthy. But there needs to be some reason why no one knows him. I'd suggest that he's English. Perhaps he moved here recently to further his father's international real estate interests. Something along those lines."

I nodded, then moved back to the group.

The women were talking about their hunting. Mrs. James Vandecourt had shot a doe, which she intended to "donate to some of the colored people around here." Mrs. Jimmy Dale Knight had bagged a six-point buck. Several others had stories.

For a while I just listened.

"What about *you*, Sunny?" Mrs. Walter Shore said. "I get the impression you're some kind of Amazon huntress." She waved her hand. "Y'all, Martha tells me she's a *bow*hunter!"

This drew a round of oohs and ahs, which—using my secret Southern woman decoder ring—I recognized as indicating that bowhunting was considered to be somewhat tacky and low class by these women.

"Well, no luck today, I'm afraid," I said. "I passed up a couple of does. But I did see a really interesting buck."

"That's why I don't bowhunt," Mrs. Jimmy Dale Knight said. "How I am—if I see it, I just flat shoot it."

Everyone laughed. Huntress humor, man, it kills me.

"Well, Sunny, spill it!" Mrs. Tommy Hathaway said. "Tell us about your buck."

"Huge rack," I said, drawing on Gunnar Brushwood's coaching. "Nontypical. Must have had twenty points. Couple of drop tines, so many stickers I couldn't even count."

The women stared at me blank faced. I couldn't figure out what I'd said.

"Also. It was white."

Jaws dropped. Finally Mrs. James Vandecourt—a tall woman with tastefully faked blond hair and the sort of breasts that don't appear in nature—picked up a cocktail fork, and binged it on the side of her glass until the room was silent. "Y'all!" she said, putting her long bony arm around my shoulder. "Y'all, I just want everybody to know that this miserable little person here, our newest member, Mrs. Rodney Childs, in her *first* day of hunting at Hellespont Lodge ..." She waved her drink around. "No, no, listen up, y'all! Sunny Childs here, she just saw Moby Dick, the great white deer!"

Several women gasped. "Moby *Dick*!" someone whispered. Then the room descended into reverent silence for a while. Finally, after a few more seconds, Mrs. James Vandecourt began clapping, and the entire room began to applaud.

I grinned and waved.

When the hubbub had settled down, Mrs. James Vandecourt said, "Moby Dick is a legend here. Nobody's seen him for years. We all figured he must be dead by now."

"Some of the ladies here would *kill* to get a shot at him," Mrs. Tommy Hathaway said.

"Y'all? Y'all? *I* saw him, y'all," Mrs. Walter Shore said. "Four years ago. He must be fifteen years old by now. Didn't have the heart to shoot him."

"Didn't have the *heart* to shoot him." Mrs. Jimmy Dale Knight rolled her eyes. She was younger than the others, about my age, with large collagen-enhanced lips, gym-toned arms, a big head of natural blond hair, and a voice that was like nails on a chalkboard. There was something slightly less refined than the others about her, a bitchy quality that she seemed to take pleasure in displaying. "Meaning what, honey? You shot at him and missed?"

Mrs. Walter Shore laughed and winked at me. "Might could be."

There was a lull in the conversation, so I seized the opportunity to get some work done. "Speaking of which," I said, "wasn't someone shot in this room last year?"

There was a brief silence. The four women looked at me with pitying eyes. As usual, Miss Tactful had stuck her foot in it. Apparently I'd breached some unwritten rule of lodge etiquette.

With a strained smile, Mrs. James Vandecourt said, "Such a loss. Such a sad thing."

"She was just the *sweetest* girl," Mrs. Walter Shore said, a fairly perfunctory note in her voice.

More uncomfortable silence. But then I figured, screw it, I was here to do a job, not win a popularity contest. "What do you think happened to her?" I said.

The four women looked at each other warily. "Honey, you know, it just feels a little un*seemly* talking about it in this room."

"Macabre," Mrs. Walter Shore said. She had coal black hair, and an obliging expression on her face. Trying to help ease me out of an embarrassing situation.

"Tacky!" said Mrs. Jimmy Dale Knight snippily. "It's just plain out *tacky* talking about it."

I decided to pretend I was my mother, the master of eyelash batting and false smiles. "You think so?" I said. I batted my eyelashes, gave them my best, widest, dumbest, cow-eyed expression, then smiled as brightly and guilelessly as I was capable. "I just think it's so creepy. And so *fascinating*."

There was a brief moment where the matter hung in the balance. And suddenly the momentum shifted and the whole conversation tipped my way. All four of the women moved an inch or two toward me, their voices dropped, and their eyes took on a conspiratorial gleam.

"Bless her heart," Mrs. James Vandecourt said, hardly moving her lips.

"Bless her heart," Mrs. Walter Shore said.

"Not to speak ill of the dead . . ."

"Oh, bless her heart, no!" Mrs. Walter Shore said.

"I am *certainly* not one to speak ill of the dead."

"Oh, my Lord, no!"

"But—"

"But . . ."

"But . . ."

"But!" Mrs. Tommy Hathaway dipped her chin half an inch and rested two long-nailed fingers on her carefully depilated upper lip.

"Mm-hm," Mrs. James Vandecourt said. "I feel she took wrongful advantage of her situation here."

"Really?" I said, giving her some FASCINATED! with my eyes and some JUST A LITTLE SCANDAL-IZED! with my lower lip.

"Entre nous, of course." Mrs. James Vandecourt's sniff was barely audible. "I am told by a reliable source that she actually tried to *borrow money* from a certain member of this lodge."

"Oh my *God*!" Mrs. Jimmy Dale Knight said. "That is so *tacky*."

"Not only *that*, when this certain person refused, the dearly departed actually had the gall to threaten to expose certain unseemly facts from said person's past."

This resulted in a hushed silence.

Mrs. Walter Shore leaned forward. "I have never told this to a *soul.* But she did the same thing to me."

Pregnant silence.

"Me, also," Mrs. Tommy Hathaway said, her voice barely audible.

I looked at Mrs. James Vandecourt. She gave me a knowing look, intimating without a word that she, too, had been approached.

I turned to Mrs. Jimmy Dale Knight. "You?"

Mrs. Jimmy Dale Knight curled her collagenated lip slightly. "All right. All right. All right, y'all." Then, in a voice so low it was almost a hiss: "I told her, 'Girl, you better step off or I'm gonna put six hundred dollars' worth of Eyetalian leather right up your dirty, chiseling little ass."

I expected the other women to look a little off-put by the earthiness of this remark, but they didn't seem to be. Instead they all crinkled their eyes, and smiled without showing their teeth.

"You're saying she actually tried to blackmail people in this group?" I said.

"Blackmail!" All eyebrows shot up. "Oh, that's putting it a little *strong.*"

"Oh, that's *entirely* too strong!"

Again, I figured in for a penny, in for a pound. I made pouty lips, then gave a little flirty waggle with my head and leaned forward conspiratorially. "So?" I let my eyes go wide and my voice drop to a whisper. "Did any of y'all pay?"

I was surprised when, instead of vehement denials, the women all eyed each other uncomfortably.

"Sunny," Mrs. Jimmy Dale Knight said in her high, harsh voice, "you gonna have to learn, there's some questions around here you just don't ask."

"Oh, I know, I *know*!" I did my best Southern sorority girl twang, gave Mrs. Walter Shore a playful little swat on the elbow. "I'm so bad. I'm terrible. I'm terrible, y'all."

"You are!"

"You are *terrible*!"

"You are *awful*, Sunny!" Mrs. James Vandecourt leaned toward me, pressing the tips of her fingers flat against my shoulder. "You are just a *horrible* little creature. You gonna fit *right* in around here!"

I batted my eyelashes, and then we all laughed and laughed. Sometimes I scare myself. And I had to wonder. What *kind* of questions did you not ask around here? What did she mean by that?

CHAPTER 9

AFTER DINNER I went up to my room. About nine someone knocked on the door. It was Martha Herrington. She was wearing the same floor-length black cloak that she had been wearing the night before. She had another piece of heavy black fabric draped over her arm. I noticed her feet were bare.

"I forgot to mention, Sunny," she said. "There's a silly little ceremonial event that we do. Inducting new members, that sort of thing."

"Oh, okay. Do I need to get dressed up or anything?"

She shook her head. "Just this." She handed me the black fabric. It turned out to be a cloak, too, made of heavy black velvet.

"What about underneath?" I said.

Martha Herrington raised her eyebrows in comical fashion, leaned toward me slightly, then popped her robe open just long enough for me to see that she was naked underneath. She laughed loudly. "It's just tradition. The whole thing won't even last long enough for you to get cold."

"Okay," I said dubiously.

• • •

Ten minutes later I was standing in the dark hallway outside the Georgia Room—the largest room in the lodge, according to Martha Herrington. Next to me was a young woman, her lustrous black hair and bland, pretty face barely visible in the light of a single torch hanging from a bracket on the wall.

"I am *so* nervous," she said. "God, I feel like it's rush week all over."

"I'm afraid I missed the whole rush thing," I said. "No sororities where I went to school."

"You poor thing," she said. Then, in a hushed voice, she said, "I hear the induction is really *creepy*."

Before I had a chance to respond, the iron-hinged double doors in front of us groaned open.

The Georgia Room was lit only by candles and by a big fire roaring in the massive fireplace at the end of the room. A makeshift platform, reminiscent of an altar, had been erected at the far end of the room. On each side of the room was a row of black-robed figures, their faces hidden behind black masks.

"Enter!" intoned the woman who stood on the platform. I recognized by the voice that it was Martha Herrington. In addition to the black cloak and the black mask, she was distinguished from the other women in that she wore a black hood. It all seemed a little over-the-top to me, like something from a KKK rally.

"When in Rome," I mouthed to my companion.

She swallowed nervously. As we walked slowly into the room, a low noise began to rise around us. It took me a moment to realize that it was the women in the black robes, singing. The song had an odd tune, ancient-sounding and angular, with no words that I could distinguish. For the first time, I began to feel a little nervous.

Behind us the doors boomed shut, and the strange chorus faded.

"Sisters!" called Martha Herrington. "We gather again on this night, in memory of the act of sacrifice by which this lodge was founded, in recognition of the deep and secret bond which ties us, and in celebration of the addition of two new members to our Sisterhood."

The dark chorus began another wordless minor key chant.

"The act of sacrifice!" she said.

"The act of sacrifice," the women responded.

"The bond of blood!"

"The bond of blood."

Martha Herrington reached behind her and picked up a thin stick of wood, with a string dangling from it. As she bent the stick across her bare knee, I realized it was a bow. "The bow restrung!"

"The bow restrung."

She lifted the bow she had just strung, nocked an arrow, pulled the bow back. For a moment I thought she was aiming it right at me. My heart raced.

"The arrow loosed!"

"The arrow loosed."

She released the arrow, which flew between me and the young woman with the glossy black hair. The arrow stuck in the big wooden door with a solid thunk. Suddenly I felt angry. That was a real arrow! If she had hiccuped, Martha Herrington could have easily spitted me to the door.

"Let us join, Sisters, to offer sacrifice!"

The chanting began again. Martha Herrington picked up what appeared to me to be a deer skull off the podium next to her, poured something into it from a gold flask.

"Devotees! Approach!"

It took me a moment to realize that she meant that I and the black-haired young woman were supposed to come to the makeshift altar. I walked up and stood in front of her.

"Kneel."

We knelt.

The chanting had become louder, more insistent. But not so loud as to muffle the sound of bare feet coming up behind us.

"Acolytes . . ." Martha gestured to whoever had come up from behind us. I felt a pair of hands on my shoulders and suddenly the black robe—which was all that separated me from nakedness—was slipped off my shoulders.

"Hey, shit!" I said. I couldn't help myself. "Oops, sorry."

The black-haired young woman tittered nervously as her robe fell. Martha Herrington gave her a hard glance and the tittering stopped. I'm not someone who feels especially self-conscious about my body, but this was more than a little off-putting. It's moments like these when you start thinking that being a private investigator is one of your dumber career moves.

"With this and this alone do we enter the world!" Martha Herrington made a cheesy, theatrical gesture with the deer skull, taking in our naked bodies. "This is our treasure."

"This is our treasure."

She then raised the deer skull over her head. "Repeat after me, Devotees! With this sacrifice . . ."

"With this sacrifice." It was just me and the dark-haired girl repeating the words now.

"I shall rise."

"I shall rise."

"In the name of all that is holy, I promise . . ."

"In the name of all that is holy, I promise . . ."

". . . that I shall not reveal . . ."

"That I shall not reveal."

". . . the secret bond which joins us, sister to sister . . ."

"The secret bond which humma humma, sister to sister." I've never been good at the whole repeat-after-me thing. I seem only to be able to hold about six words in my head at a time.

"Soul to soul . . ."

"Soul to soul."

". . . generation to generation . . ."

"Generation to generation."

"The conquest of the dark beast is our sacrament . . ."

"The conquest of the dark beast is our sacrament."

". . . and our goal."

"And our goal."

"As we loose the arrow and pierce the heart, we join that which we destroy."

"We shall loose the humma humma humma humma, we join that which we destroy."

She lowered the deer skull and put it to my lips.

"Drink, Devotee!" she commanded, tipping the deer skull toward me.

I drank from the skull. It was a thick, warm, salty-tasting drink. Martha—intentionally, I think—poured it too fast. I choked and the liquid ran down my face and neck and down my bare skin. She pulled the deer skull away, and I saw then that it was blood, blood pouring down my bare flesh in red-black rivulets. I felt like an extra in that movie *Carrie,* where Sissy Spacek blows up the high school dance after the bitchy cheerleaders pour blood on her head.

I gagged. Martha repeated the process with my raven-haired compatriot, who also got a chest full of gore for her trouble. She had arched her back a little, I couldn't help but notice, the better to show off a pair of breasts far too perky to have grown there naturally.

The chanting began again, and the cloaks were placed back on our backs, covering us.

"Rise!" Martha said.

We stood.

"Welcome, Sisters!"

"Welcome, Sisters!

"Let never our bonds asunder break."

"Let never our bonds asunder break."

After that there was some more ceremonial nonsense. One of the other black-robed women gave Martha Herrington a silver cup with the word TRUTH engraved on the side, and somebody read a long poem about hunting.

Then we were called up to the front and told to kneel for a second time. Martha Herrington fixed her black eyes on each of us for a long moment. The chanting began again, and the two lines of black-clad women filed slowly out of the room.

The room was finally silent, except for the snapping of wood in the fire.

"Is that it?" I said.

"Not unless you girls have a problem joining us for cocktails in the Whitetail Room," Martha Herrington said, no longer in her high priestess tone of voice.

"Oh, my Lord!" the black-haired woman gushed after Martha had left the room. "That was the most *intense* thing I have ever *done* in my life."

"Lucky you," I muttered.

"Like I said, Sunny, just a silly old tradition." It was Martha Herrington talking to me, unmasked and unhooded, but still wearing her black robe. The ladies were all around us in their black robes, drinking out of highball glasses, laughing, joking. Martha was drinking scotch out of the silver cup she'd been given during the ceremony, the one that said TRUTH on the side.

"What's the silver cup represent?" I said.

She held it up to the light. "Just something I did for the club. It's not really part of the ceremony per se."

"Wasn't there a line in the ceremony, something about the act of sacrifice which founded the lodge?" I said. "What was that all about?" I was remembering what Rochelle Longineau, Sheriff Timmers's nurse, had told me about the woman who inherited the lodge after blowing her husband's head off.

She swatted the air in front of me. "Oh, just a bunch of hooey. The girls who founded this place back in the twenties wanted it to be like the Masons. You know, ancient and mysterious. It's just fun, doesn't mean a thing."

I nodded. "So look, Martha, I meant to ask you, have you tracked down the lodge membership list for me? I wanted to cross-reference everything, figure out which members were in the lodge, which weren't, that sort of thing."

Martha Herrington looked at me blankly. "List?"

"The other night? Remember? I asked you for a list of members."

"Hm. Yes. Well, you see that might be a problem. We really do try to keep that list confidential."

I felt puzzled. "Wait, I thought we already got this cleared up the other night. My report to you, my findings, whatever this investigation turns up—it's all confidential. *You* hired me. So if I'm going to do my job here, I need that list."

Martha Herrington sighed, showing me some annoyance. "Well, I just don't think that's possible." She smiled brightly.

"What do you mean, it's not possible? You're refusing to give me a list of suspects?"

"Suspects! That seems to be going an extra yard or two, don't you think?"

"Do you want me to do this or not?"

Martha's expensive teeth kept gleaming at me. "Sunny, we hired you for your discretion. There will simply have to be certain parameters in your investigation. Mingle, talk, circulate, chat up the help—whatever you need to do of that nature. But I can't have you dredging up all kinds of information, willy-nilly, about people who are uninvolved in this matter. It's that simple."

I started to get mad. But then I thought about where I was. It's not a question I often ask myself, but what I figured was: what would my mother do if she were in my shoes? The answer was, smile. My mother, standing in my shoes, would smile . . . and then she'd go and do whatever she wanted.

I smiled. "Martha, honey," I said, "I get so wrapped up in things, sometimes I forget myself. Consider the matter closed."

I patted her arm and went off to bed.

It was the first chance I'd had to go over the case file I'd gotten from Agent Allgood. I sat down at the little desk in my room, turned on the lamp, and began reading. It was a discouragingly thin file.

The autopsy revealed very little beyond what Allgood had already told me. Jennifer Treadaway was a 42-year-old female in good health, 5 foot 9, 137 pounds. Cause of death, exsanguination due to a single stab wound. The cutting implement—presumably a knife—had entered the neck in the front, gone through both the carotid artery and the jugular vein, nicked the second cervical vertebra, and partially severed the spinal cord. No evidence of beating, restraint, or sexual assault, no defensive wounds. The feet had been washed in bleach.

Witness reports had been taken from twelve women—including Martha Herrington, all five women I'd spoken with earlier in the day . . . and my mother. The witness reports all contained the same phrase: *the subject indicated she had slept through the night and didn't hear any sort of altercation or struggle.*

I got on the phone and called my mom. It was ten-thirty by then—but my mom is a night owl. "You haven't called in weeks, Sunny," she said. "I have just been about to *die* with anxiety. What's wrong?"

"Nothing's wrong," I said.

"Something's wrong or you wouldn't have called me."

"Barrington and I have just been going through a rough patch, that's all. He went down to Barbados without me."

That brought on a brief silence. Mom is torn on the matter of Barrington. Barrington is black, he's a cop, and he's nowhere near rich. For a person like Mom, all of the above are strikes against him. But in spite of herself, she likes him better than anybody else I've gone out with. There is a decency about Barrington that even somebody like my mother can't help but respond to.

"Anyway, look, Mom, I'm not calling to talk about Barrington. The reason I called, I'm down here at the Hellespont Lodge . . ."

"You're *what*?"

"I'm at the Hellespont Lodge."

There was a long silence. "For goodness' sake, why?"

"You remember last year when Jennifer Treadaway got murdered. Martha Herrington has hired me to investigate."

Mom is not the silent type. But this seemed to have struck her dumb.

"So, look, Mom, the reason I called, I wanted to get your thoughts about her murder, see if you knew anything about her."

There was a brief silence, then Mom said, in her coolest of tones, "Sweetie, now why would you be doing a thing like that?"

"It's my job."

Big sigh. "Sometimes I just *despair* of you."

"What does that have to do with Jennifer Treadaway?"

Mom is the master of the oblique answer. "Well, honey, I was asleep all night. I didn't hear a *thing*. As you know, I'm a late sleeper."

"Okay, forget about the killing itself. Tell me about Jennifer Treadaway."

"We weren't close," Mom said. "Of course we moved in the same circles. She was a lovely woman, I'm sure . . ."

"But . . ."

"Oh, nothing, nothing."

Mom infuriates me. "Mom, don't *nothing nothing* me. You obviously have something to say about her."

"Oh well, it's not anything in *particular*. But I have to say, my impression of her was that she lacked a certain refinement."

"Sort of like me?"

Mom cleared her throat—hem—like they used to teach rich girls in elocution class. "No, not like you at all. God help me, whatever I did wrong in educating you, I'll be the first to admit that Sunny Childs is a what-you-see-is-what-you-get person. I admire that, really I do. No, the thing about Jennifer is that she seemed to be working so *hard* all the time. Refinement must, above all, appear effortless. Effortless is the very soul of grace. Poor Jennifer never understood that."

"You would have made a great geisha, Mom."

"Is that one of your backhanded compliments, dear? Or do you just enjoy insulting me?"

"Forget it. I'm just trying to find out about Jennifer Treadaway. Could you, for once in your life, just skip the nicey-nice folderol and tell me what you know?" This is how it always goes with me and my mother. She plays the lady of refinement, and then my voice starts getting loud.

"Sunny, I do not now, nor will I ever, understand your obsession with seeing the ugliness of the world. But if you want the ugliness, here it is. Jennifer Treadaway married Arvin Treadaway when she was twenty-five, and at that point she became fabulously wealthy and had everything in the world. But she was born in a trailer park in Macon. Her mother was a truckstop prostitute. Her father was killed by another inmate down at the Reidsville pen after he was convicted of molesting his own daughter. These are the ugly facts. And Jennifer, she couldn't seem to shake them."

"Are you saying she was killed because of her past?"

"I have not the faintest idea why she was killed. And quite frankly I'm not eager to find out."

"That's all you can tell me?"

"What I *would* tell you—if I thought it would have the slightest impression upon your hard little head—is that I think you ought to call Barrington up, apologize, and then take the next plane to whatever island he's on." A long, theatrical, suffering sigh. "But of course, you never listen to me."

"You don't want me investigating this case."

"Mercy! I never said that! One has priorities, that's all. It saddens me that you would value a paycheck over a man who loves you."

"You're one to talk." I slammed the phone down in her ear before she got a chance to get the last word in.

I plowed through the rest of the case file. It was clear that Allgood hadn't been confident he even knew everybody who had been at the lodge that night— much less who might have had a motive for murdering Jennifer Treadaway.

The one thing that piqued my interest was a brief interview with Arvin Treadaway, Jennifer's husband. According to Allgood's notes, he had talked to Treadaway at the headquarters of Treadaway Properties in Atlanta. Here was the entirety of the witness report:

Subject very distraught. Indicated he and victim had been married for seventeen years. She was his second wife. Two children. Subject claimed he was on business trip to New York City on the night of the murder, staying in room 417 at Plaza Hotel. (This investigator later confirmed validity of this statement.) When asked about victim's background, subject responded that prior to their marriage the deceased had resided in Staunton, Virginia, where her father was commandant of a military academy. She had graduated Sweetbriar College. Both parents were deceased. He was unable to produce any motive or possible suspect for killing.

And that was it. The reason it interested me was that it conflicted with what my mother had said. My mother is not particularly wedded to the truth. But I doubted she would claim somebody's mother was a truckstop whore from Macon, if there wasn't at least a grain of truth to the story.

I dialed Information, asked for the name of a military academy in Staunton, Virginia.

"It's pronounced STAN-ton," the operator said. "Not STAWNton."

"You're from around there?"

"Grew up in Staunton." I heard some keyboard tap-ping noises. "No military academy listed."

"You ever heard of any sort of military academy around there?" I said.

"Well, there used to be one, Staunton Military Acad-emy. Up on a big hill above town. But that place shut down a million years ago."

"Thanks." I hung up, then flipped to the last page of the file.

It was a plaintive note from Agent Allgood.

FILE MEMORANDUM

It is the belief of the undersigned agent that this case has been intentionally interfered with by powerful persons who may or may not be connected directly to the murder itself. It is possible their motives may be simply an avoidance of embarrassment. I am in no position to speculate. I have protested to my superiors about the disposition and handling of this case, but to no avail. When I attempted to receive authorization to discipline lodge members and staff for tampering with evidence, I received instruction from my superiors not to pursue such avenues. If any subsequent investigator should attempt to reopen this investigation, all I have to say is Good Luck.

[signed] Wayne Algood
Special Agent
Georgia Bureau of Investigation

On that cheery note, I went to bed.

CHAPTER 10

AT AROUND ONE-THIRTY in the morning, I woke up to an eerie howling. It took me a while in my groggy state to figure out what it was. Coyotes. I tried to sleep, but the noise gave me the creeps. As I was lying around thinking about the case, an idea struck me.

I got up, put on my robe, and slipped downstairs, through several hallways, until I was standing in front of a door labeled OFFICE.

Out of the pocket of my robe I pulled a small device that looked like an electric screwdriver, but instead of a screw shank it had small steel prongs and a thin steel hook on the end. I inserted the prongs and the hook into the lock, applied a little clockwise pressure, and then hit a red button on the body of the machine. The electric lock pick emitted a loud buzz, the doorknob vibrated, and then the knob suddenly turned. I was in!

I put the electric lock pick back in my pocket, closed the door as softly as I could—though the hinges groaned loudly—and then probed the room with a small Maglite. I locked the door and then began the search.

It was an ordinary little office, cheap desk and chair from Office Depot, a computer, a gray filing cabinet, and one of the lodge's omnipresent dead deer staring mournfully at me from the wall.

I searched the filing cabinet for files containing membership roles, but it was mostly information on tax filings, receipts, and other papers of a financial nature. Next I turned on the computer.

Just as the machine came on, I heard a noise in the hall. A slow, stealthy tread. I froze. Two shadows thrown by a pair of feet moved through the strip of light under the door. The computer beeped loudly, and the two shadows stopped moving.

After a moment I heard a jingle of keys. I looked frantically around the room. There was a closet on the other side of it. I was wearing leather slippers which made a loud slapping noise on the flagstone floors. Afraid I would make a noise, I took my feet out of the slippers, padded across the room, and jumped into the closet. I had just gotten into the closet when I heard the hinges groan again. A male voice mumbled something angrily, then whoever it was crossed the room. After a few seconds I heard the click of a switch, there was another beep, then the computer's fan went silent.

After a few moments the door groaned again and the light went off. I looked at my watch in the gloom. One-fifteen A.M. I waited silently, my heart banging in my chest, until one-thirty. Then I stealthily opened the door. Silence.

I crossed the room, opened the hallway door, peeped out. Nobody there.

I went back inside, fired up the computer. It took

me about an hour of searching, but I finally found the files. After another check of the hallway, I printed up the list of members—about thirty names—turned off the computer, left the room.

I had gotten back to my room when I realized I had left my slippers downstairs. I considered going back for them, but decided that would probably be a mistake. I could slip in and get them in the morning.

My alarm went off at four. I got up blearily, threw on my camo outfit, grabbed my bow, and headed out the door.

Sitting next to the door, as though left by a maid at a fancy hotel, was a pair of leather slippers. I felt a prickling on the back of my neck as I grabbed them and threw them inside my room.

CHAPTER 11

DOWNSTAIRS A BIG topographical map was hanging on the wall of the Georgia Room, the locations of the various hunting stands indicated in red. Gunnar had told me that deer hunters were big on using topographical maps to locate productive places for blasting deer. He had given me a long explanation about wind direction and brushy bottom land and ridges and creeks and bottlenecks and stuff, but I hadn't paid a great deal of attention.

I was staring blankly at the map when someone came up behind me, reached over my shoulder, and planted a dirty finger on one of the red dots.

I turned, found my face inches away from Biggs, Horst's assistant. It was the first time I'd gotten a good look at him. Like Horst, he had an ex-military quality about him. But there was a different look in his eyes. Where Horst's eyes were secretive little slits, Biggs's were wide and staring.

"You think that's the place to go today?" I said.

Biggs didn't reply, just stared at me for a minute, his eyes running up and down my body. Then he picked up my bow and began walking down the hallway. I followed him in silence. He took me to a camouflage-colored all-terrain vehicle parked by a shed behind the lodge, indicated for me to get on the back. I got on behind him and he immediately accelerated into the night. It was obvious to me that the ATV had been modified somehow: it hardly made any sound at all as it drove through the dark trees. To avoid spooking game, I supposed. Biggs didn't turn on the lights either, riding through the blackness at a breakneck pace. I had to grab him around the chest just to keep from falling off.

"How can you see?" I said.

Biggs didn't answer.

Finally we stopped. He pointed off into the blackness. Presumably there was a stand out there somewhere.

"I can't see it."

He just kept pointing. For a moment I considered telling him to take me back to the Lodge. But since I was trying to be inconspicuous, and the scuttlebutt around the lodge was that Biggs knew the deer on the property better than anyone, I figured I'd best shut up and do as he said. Just as I picked up my bow and was about to walk out into the darkness, he spoke, his voice a hoarse whisper. It was the first time I'd ever heard him speak. "You get your shoes?"

I stared at him. In the blackness his face was invisible. "How did you know?"

"Be careful out here," he whispered. "They still haven't caught them boys that escaped from the prison the other night." Then he gunned the ATV and headed off into the dark.

●   ●   ●

I wasn't sure why, but I was feeling eager for the sun to come up. Curiosity, maybe. It was still half an hour before sunup, so I just sat there in the cool fall air and let my eyes acclimate to the dark. Once the sky started to grow pale, I took an arrow out of the quiver, nocked it, and sat with the bow on my lap, looking down at the ground below. I couldn't see much, though, because I was wrapped in a heavy fog.

It wasn't long before I heard noises around me—pine needles crunching, small intakes of breath. I kept staring and suddenly I saw them. I don't know if the fog had thinned or the light increased or my eyes just got used to the murky view—but there they were: ten or fifteen deer, all of them clustered around a huge water oak thirty or forty yards to my left, eating acorns off the ground. Does, fawns, even a couple of spike-horned yearling bucks. I could hear the crunching of acorns in their mouths, an occasional discharge of breath.

I watched them graze, admiring their alertness. They were kind of neurotic animals, always peeping around, their eyes darting from side to side. Gunnar had made me shoot at a variety of distances, calculating a maximum range from which I ought to shoot. It hadn't meant much to me since I had no intention of shooting anything . . . but still, it had gotten me in the habit of calculating distance. The nearest doe was twenty-five yards away, just outside my range.

Then, from behind the tree stepped a big buck, an eight-pointer. The wind shifted momentarily, the fog thickened, and the buck disappeared. When the fog thinned again a few seconds later, the buck was closer. Twenty-five yards and closing. It paused, put its head down to retrieve an acorn. Then up again and walking. Twenty yards, eighteen, fifteen.

It paused again, turned broadside to me, put its head down.

Without thinking, I lifted my bow, sighted on its flank. The deer's head jerked up and it looked around nervously. I froze. Several of the other deer, picking up on the buck's nervousness, looked around, too. Gunnar had told me that deer were color-blind, that they didn't distinguish shape so much as they did movement. But smell was their best defense. A slight wind riffled the hair around my face, blowing my scent away from the buck below me. I sat motionless for what must have been five minutes. My heart was beating fast as a triphammer and my hands trembled. Finally the nervous buck put his head down for another acorn.

I drew my arrow, pulled the kisser button to the corner of my mouth, let the fifteen-yard pin drop to the circle just behind the buck's front shoulder. And in that moment I was aware that my hands had suddenly steadied, that my heart had slowed, that a sensation of deep pleasure and calm had coursed through my chest.

"Are you out of your mind?" I said loudly.

The deer turned a hundred and eighty degrees, its white tail went up like a flag, and then the whole herd was bounding into the woods, their hooves crashing in the pine needles.

The arrow was still aimed at the spot where the buck's heart and lungs had been just seconds before. A pine cone lay on the ground exactly where I was aiming.

I let my fingers grow relaxed, released the arrow. It

arced through the air, with a solid thump, embedded itself in the ground. The pine cone shattered, split in half.

Then the forest was completely silent.

I pulled a map out of my backpack, climbed down from the tree, and began walking. I quickly found the path, rutted by ATV tracks, began following it back in the direction of the lodge.

I'd gone half a mile or so, past an overgrown section of clearcut and into a stand of planted pine, when I heard the muted sound of an ATV coming toward me. Biggs? I didn't feel like having him ask why I had left my stand so early in the morning, so I ducked back into some bushes at the side of the path.

The ATV came up over a rise, and swept past me. As I anticipated, it was Biggs. There was a fork just a hundred yards or so back down the path, and he took the route that led away from the stand where I'd been that morning.

Out of curiosity, I backtracked. By the time I'd reached the fork, he was at the far side of the clearcut. I hadn't noticed earlier, but in the distance a small gravel road twisted through the woods, and next to it stood an unobtrusive metal building of the sort farmers store agricultural equipment in. Around the lodge Biggs had seemed like a clod—slow-moving, maybe a little stupid. But as he pulled up at the outbuilding, hopped off the ATV, and trotted through a steel door, there was a lightness, a quickness, to his movements that I hadn't seen around the lodge. Moments later I heard a vehicle pull out onto the gravel road. I lifted my compact field glasses, expecting I'm not sure what—maybe a ten-year-old pickup truck, or a rusting Jeep. So I was surprised to see Biggs's face on the driver's side of a shiny Mercedes sedan, one of the big ones.

Was it his? Hard to believe you could afford a big Mercedes on an assistant gamekeeper's pay. Maybe it belonged to one of the women in the club.

I began walking back toward the lodge. It was a beautiful day, clear and crisp, the fog all gone now. I felt an unfamiliar pleasure moving in me, and I wasn't sure why.

CHAPTER 12

I LEFT THE lodge at around eight, stopped for two cups of coffee, reached the GBI Macon office just in time to find Agent Allgood's worn cowboy boot emerging from his state-owned white Ford sedan.

"Morning!" I called to him, holding out a Starbucks cup. "Hope you like cream and sugar."

He eyed me for a moment, then took the cup. "Let me ask you this," he said. "How come when I was investigating, none of these rich folks from Atlanta seemed to want this thing solved. Now, a year later, all of a sudden they do? That seem strange to you?"

"I don't know enough yet to even guess."

"You want to come inside?"

"I've just got something quick for you," I said. I handed him a list of names, all the employees at the lodge. "You think you could run these through the crime computer?"

"I already ran the employees," he said sharply. "I told you I came up dry."

"You did? It's not in the file."

He raised his eyebrows. "It's not?"

I shook my head.

"Huh. Well, like I say, I didn't come up with nothing," he said. "The employees are clean."

"You mind doing it again?"

"I told you that—"

"Indulge me," I said. "Please? Who knows, maybe one of them has done something since, something that didn't show up when you ran them last year."

He grabbed the list of employees out of my hand, glared at it. I handed him a business card with the phone number of the Hellespont Lodge on it.

"Call me when you're done."

According to the investigation file, Jennifer Treadaway's maiden name was Poythruss. Not the most common name in the world, I figured. But then when I pulled open a phone book at a pay phone down at the mall, I found at least three dozen entries for people of that name in the vicinity of Macon. I had plenty of time, so I drove down to the county courthouse, took a peek through their criminal files. The Poythrusses of Macon were apparently a family of great criminal propensity. There were sixteen Poythrusses with convictions on this list. Of those, however, only two were women. One had been convicted of a number of drug offenses ranging from simple possession all the way up to trafficking, while the other had one conviction for solicitation of prostitution. I wrote down both names.

I called the prostitute first, Rolanda Poythruss, but the line was busy. So just for yucks I called the first name, Jolyne Poythruss, the one busted for drugs and assault.

A woman answered, sounding sleepy and put out, like I'd woken her.

"Sorry to disturb you," I said, "but are you Jennifer Treadaway's mother?"

"Hell no!" the woman said, slamming down the phone.

I frowned, hit redial. "Me again," I said. "You wouldn't happen to know who Jennifer Treadaway is. She used to be Jennifer Poythruss."

"I'm trying to sleep," the woman said.

"I apologize. But it sounded from your response like maybe you knew Jennifer."

"That slut's my sister," the woman said finally.

"Really? Look, my name is Sunny Childs. I'm an investigator from Atlanta. Could I come out and ask you a few questions about your sister's death?"

"Seem like can't nobody get no sleep around here."

Half an hour later I was pulling into a trailer park smack in the flight path of the Macon Airport. As I banged on the flimsy door of a battered trailer at the back of the lot, a single-engine jet was wobbling into the air a few hundred feet above me.

A bleary-looking woman with stringy blond hair and a massive bruise that had swollen her left eye shut opened the door. She looked about sixty, but I suspect she was probably closer to forty. "Private investigator, huh?"

I nodded.

"Well. Come on in. I guess." The woman with the bruised face shut the door behind me, and I walked in. The trailer stank of sweat, collard greens, and marijuana.

"I'm Sunny Childs," I said, sitting on a plaid couch, with grimy foam erupting from large holes in the armrests.

"Jolyne," she said. "But I guess you already know that." She lit a cigarette, looked suspiciously at my camouflage outfit. "You in the army or something?"

"No, I was just out hunting."

"Oh. Then who hired you to find out about Jennifer? Insurance company or something?"

I shook my head. "I'm afraid that's confidential."

"Oh, well, *exsqueeze* me." She waved the cigarette la-di-da fashion in the air, her pinky finger sticking out.

"Look, it's nothing personal, that's just how we have to do it."

Jolyne looked sly. "You think they's any money in it for, uh, members of her family? From insurance or something?"

"Very possibly," I said.

Jolyne brightened considerably. "What you want to know?"

"When was the last time you saw your sister?" I said.

"I'd say about 1983," she said.

I must have looked surprised.

"I was locked up for a stretch," she said. "I didn't see her up to the time she got kilt."

"You hear from her since then?"

"She wrote me a couple times in the penitentiary, but that was about it."

"So you haven't seen or heard from your sister since she moved to Atlanta?"

Jolyne blinked. "Huh?"

"Since she moved to Atlanta, you haven't heard from her?"

"I don't know what you talking about."

I sighed. So this was looking like a dead end. Obviously she hadn't been in touch with her sister at all since Jennifer made the leap out of the lower classes. "Look, it sounds like I'm not going to get what I need from you. Is there anybody else in the family that might have seen her between the time that she left Macon and the time she was murdered?"

Jolyne's eyes narrowed. *"Murdered?"*

"That's what we're talking about, right?"

"Murdered? Jennifer wasn't murdered."

Suddenly I got a peculiar feeling. I opened my file, took out the portrait of Jennifer Treadaway, handed it to her without speaking.

Jolyne scowled as she peered at the photograph. "That ain't Jennifer."

"Oh, my God," I said. "I'm so embarrassed. I can't believe I've got the wrong person." I stood, put my hand out for the picture.

Jolyne didn't make any move to hand it back to me. Instead she just kept staring at the picture. "The fucking bitch," she said finally.

"What do you mean?" I said.

Jolyne smiled slightly. "By God, don't she look different, though!"

"Who?"

Jolyne took a drag on her cigarette, tapped the photo with her fingernail. "The chick in this picture? Her name's Terry White. She was my cellmate when I was in the penitentiary back in '82."

I felt a coldness draining down my neck.

"I bet that bitch heard me talking about how my goodie-goodie little sister done got hit by that car. Soon as she got out, she must of just took over Jennifer's identity."

"This Terry, what was she in for?" I said.

Jolyne tossed the picture on the coffee table next to a stained Plexiglas water pipe. "Terry? Shoot, man, she kilt her husband with a hatchet."

I picked up the photograph, looked at it with renewed interest.

"So Terry, she got murdered? That what you saying?"

I nodded.

"Serves her right." Jolyne dropped her cigarette into the mouth of the bong. It hissed as it hit the water.

I got up and headed for the door. As I was leaving, Jolyne stuck her head out of the trailer. "So, I don't guess there's no *in*surance money in this for me, huh?"

CHAPTER 13

THE NEXT MORNING I went out to a stand near the metal building where I'd seen Biggs the day before. The stand was perfectly situated so I could keep an eye on the metal building with my binoculars. I saw no deer. But I did see Biggs. Just as he had the previous day, he scooted by on his ATV around eight-thirty, went into the metal building, then drove off down the gravel road in a big new Mercedes.

As soon as he was gone, I climbed down from the stand and hiked over to the metal building. It was a windowless structure about thirty feet wide and close to a hundred feet long. On one of the long walls were four large bays with steel doors that rolled up into the ceiling, each of them big enough to admit a good-sized truck. I tried all the doors but they were locked.

As I was walking around the perimeter of the building, I heard the sound of a propeller-driven plane growing closer and closer to where I was standing. I was a little surprised when it passed over my head not more than a hundred feet off the ground. I continued my examination of the area around the building. Outside was a small shed with a tractor parked next to it. A rusting harrow, a seeder, a bailer, and some other attachments for the tractor lay on the weedy ground in no particular order.

I checked the door to the shed. Also locked. Nothing seemed out of the ordinary, though. A few minutes later the small plane came back over my head again. It appeared that it had landed somewhere nearby and was taking off. As I watched, it gained altitude and disappeared off into the distance.

From down the road I heard a rumble of tires on gravel, so I headed briskly off into some bushes on a nearby hillside. Biggs arrived again, but now there was somebody else in the car, somebody whose face was obscured from my view. A bay door clattered open, apparently on remote control, the car drove in, and the bay door closed behind it. A few minutes later, one of the other doors opened, a white package truck backed out with Biggs at the wheel and a second person—whose face I still couldn't make out—sitting in the passenger's seat. Soon the truck was gone, and everything was silent.

When I got back to the lodge, several more dead deer were hanging upside down behind the meat processing room, steel gambrels hooked through their hocks, blood running out their noses and mouths. Biggs was cleaning one of them, hosing out its body cavity, a gut pile at his feet.

"Hey, Biggs," I called cheerfully.

He eyed me for a moment, continued his work without speaking.

"Too busy to say hi?" I said.

Biggs released the handle of the nozzle and the water

stopped spraying. There were flecks of blood on his face. He wiped his unshaven chin on his sleeve. "No offense, ma'am," he said. He was looking off into the distance, not meeting my eye. "The help here is encouraged not to speak to members."

"None taken," I said. "Nice buck. Who took that one?"

"Mrs. Hathaway."

I just kept standing there, seeing if he'd talk.

Finally he said, "Still no luck, huh?"

"I'm waiting on a big'un," I said. "No point blasting everything that moves."

He started spraying out the deer again.

"So, Biggs, is that your first name or your last?"

"Last."

"You have a first name?"

He made me wait awhile. "Raiford," he said.

"You ever get nervous around here?" I said.

"What?" He turned off the hose again, looking annoyed.

"Nervous. You ever get—"

"Nervous? Why would I get nervous?"

"I don't know. That nice lady got murdered last year, they never caught the killer, you're out here in the middle of nowhere all year?" I shrugged. "That doesn't make you nervous?"

"Nope." He turned his back to me now.

"Why not?"

He stopped spraying the deer. "You ask a lot of questions, don't you?"

"Hey, I'm just a Chatty Cathy I guess." I gave him a big smile.

He pointed the dribbling nozzle of the hose toward

my feet. "All this mud here, you leave footprints," he said.

"Sorry?" I looked at the ground. The impression of my boots was all over the mud.

"See, I'm looking at your footprints in this here mud, looks like about a size six, very unusual tread pattern."

"And . . ."

He looked me in the face for the first time. His eyes were black and vaguely threatening. "Sprinkled a little last night. Softened up the ground." He smiled, not in a friendly way, showing off a set of snaggled teeth. "What, Mrs. Childs, you think I wouldn't of noticed your footprints all over the place down there at the shed?"

"Look, I don't—"

Biggs lowered his voice. "Nervous? Hell, no, I'm not nervous. Reason I ain't nervous, I ain't poking my nose where it don't belong."

"Is that some kind of threat?" I said.

An odd expression passed across his face. "Not a threat, ma'am. A warning." Then he picked up a loop of deer entrails, started dragging the gut pile through the mud toward a row of garbage cans against the wall.

CHAPTER 14

A S I WENT inside, I found Martha Herrington standing in front of the lobby, hands on her hips, glaring at me. "I need to *speak* to you," she said.

"Sure," I said. "What's up?"

"Privately."

She led me down a hallway, opened the door to the lodge office. The same one I'd sneaked into the other night. After we went inside, she closed the door behind us, then picked up a sheaf of papers from the bin next to the fax machine.

"You want to tell me what *this* is?" she said, brandishing the stack of paper.

"I wouldn't have the slightest idea," I said.

"Don't lie to me, missy. It's addressed to you."

I took the papers out of her hand, looked at them. The cover sheet said it was sent to my attention from Agent Wayne Allgood of the GBI. I flipped to the next page, recognizing the format as an NCIC search file result. In other words, it was a file from the FBI's crime computer. In a flash I realized what had happened. For obvious reasons, when I go undercover, I never carry business cards. What happened was that I had scribbled my name and cell phone number on the back of a Hellespont Lodge card. Which of course, had a fax number on it. I had meant for Allgood to call me with the results of his computer search, but he had misunderstood my intent, and faxed his findings to the lodge.

I looked at the name at the top of the file. Robin Ray. Never heard of her. She wasn't one of the lodge employees whom I'd asked Agent Allgood to run through the computer. Listed beneath her name were three offenses, all of them dating back to the early eighties. Solicitation, possession with intent, loitering. I flipped to the next page. Again, it was a name I didn't recognize. The offense was a DUI in North Carolina from 1978. The third page, also a name I didn't recognize showed a conviction for manslaughter.

"I don't get it," I said. "This is some kind of mistake."

"I appreciate your zealousness on our behalf, but apparently you weren't comfortable with the parameters we asked you to honor." For the first time, Martha Herrington smiled. "Thank you *so much* for your help, Sunny, but we won't be needing your services any further."

I blinked.

She picked up the phone, dialed a number. "Horst. Mrs. Herrington. One of our members will be checking out due to an illness. Exactly. Mrs. Childs. Please send Mandy up to her room to pack her things and take them immediately down to the front entrance. And have Henry bring her car around. *Yes*, immediately. Is there something peculiar about my diction?"

She hung up the phone.

"Sunny, please go to the front lobby and wait there for your car. When it arrives, get in and drive away. I'll expect your firm to return all but, say, ten thousand of our retainer. If we do not receive the check within three business days, you'll be hearing from our attorneys."

She tried to snatch the stack of NCIC printouts from my hand, but I wheeled around and walked away before she could wrench them away from me.

I sat glumly in the lobby. The dead animals looked down at me from the high stone walls. I hadn't been fired from an engagement in years. It was my own fault, though. As soon as the client starts putting conditions on you, you just have to be tough and put your foot down. I should have resigned the engagement the second Martha Herrington started trying to hobble my investigation. I had let that fifty-thousand-dollar check color my judgment. Live and learn, I guess.

Or if you're a deer, live and get shot, then get your head glued to a wall.

A few minutes later an ancient black woman with swollen ankles and a glossy wig came hobbling down the stairs with my bags. When I hopped up and tried to help her wrestle the bags down the stairs, she looked at me like I'd blown my nose on her. So I went outside to wait.

Imagine my surprise when I saw my mother.

She was standing in the middle of the driveway, bawling orders at a horde of black men, who were carrying expensive leather bags hither and yon, taking things out of her gleaming behemoth of a Cadillac. She was wearing camouflage, head to toe, all of it terribly well tailored and flattering to her form. I wouldn't even be surprised if the camouflage baseball cap, out of which her flaming red hair appeared, had been hand made by some English tailor. I had never in my life seen Mom in camouflage: it seemed just about the most ludicrous spectacle I'd ever seen.

"What," she said, "is so terribly amusing to you?" She didn't wait for an answer, rushed over to me, gave me a big MMMOAH! MMMOAH! on each cheek. "Sunny, you look absolutely bulemic. What *have* you been eating?" Then she was back directing her minions. "Boy! Boy! Don't let that one touch the ground! It cost my husband sixteen billion lira in Milan, Italy, and I won't have it getting all scuffed up on this tacky gravel."

I cringed. The "boy" was about fifty years old. Mom's never been big on political correctness, but this whole scene seemed excessive—even for her.

At that moment the Jaguar I'd been driving swept into the drive, driven by Horst himself. He got out and opened the door for me in a gesture that managed to seem both decorous and vaguely threatening.

"Where *are* you going, Sunny?" Mom bawled. Then, pointing at Horst. "You! Drive that automobile back to wherever it came from. My daughter and I are fixing to break bread together."

Horst froze, unsure just how to handle this force of nature.

"Mom," I said, "I can't."

"Fiddlesticks!" she howled. Even for Mom, fiddlesticks is a little bit retro, a little over the top. "You and I are going to have a big fat dripping venison burger and get to the bottom of this little misunderstanding with you and Barrington."

"I said I can't."

Mom eyeballed Horst. "Is there some problem with your hearing, young man?"

"Mom! I can't stay. I got fired."

Mom's head slowly turned toward me, her eyes burning. "By *whom*?"

"Martha Herrington."

"Don't move one single *inch*," she said. Then she whirled and headed toward the lodge, her boots crunching angrily on the gravel. Just as she was about to reach the door, it opened, revealing Martha Herrington.

Martha looked a little surprised to see my mother. "Why, Miranda Wiseberg!" she said to my mother. "We weren't expecting you till next week!"

"Martha! Sweetheart, you have *lost* weight, haven't you!" my mother sang. "You look so good I could just eat you with a spoon!" Then it was MMMOAH! MMMOAH! MMMMOOOOAAAAHHI! on the cheeks, and my mother was laughing girlishly and unloading the usual torrent of lies and flattery that goes for conversation in her circle of friends. Then it was, "Martha, honey, I have just got a bone to pick with *you*!" Laugh, laugh, laugh, blink, blink, blink, titter, titter, titter.

Using a mental force field, as yet unexplained by science, my mother propelled Martha Herrington inside the doorway of the lodge. Though I couldn't hear anything, the two women were visible through the faux medieval leaded glass window. The woman my mother had been outside had been transmogrified during the intervening seconds into some kind of predatory creature: she was poking her finger in poor Martha Herrington's face and shouting things that didn't look complimentary. Martha Herrington, in turn, could do nothing but cower.

After a few minutes Martha Herrington came out by herself. Her face was pale. "You know what, honey?" she said, smiling fiercely, her accent at its drippiest, every vowel gone soft as butter in the sun. "Your mothah and I had a modest exchange of *thoughts*? And it occurred to me that perhaps I was a little *precipitous* in the decision we spoke about earlier? You just go on in and have dinnah, and I'll straighten out your belongings."

"If you say so," I said.

"Horst! Horst! What are you waiting on? Get Mrs. Childs's car back to the garage right this minute. You got more important duties at this lodge than fooling around like some little chauffeur."

CHAPTER 15

FTER THAT, I went back up to my room, still puzzled by all of the hooplah. Why had Martha Herrington flipped out when Agent Allgood had
mistakenly faxed me a bunch of crime computer files
on people who had nothing to do with the lodge?

I pulled the stack of faxes out of my purse. The
paper was wrinkled where Martha Herrington had tried
to grab them away from me. There were about thirty
or forty pages, all of them printouts from the federal
crime computer. I smoothed them out, started working
my way through them. Some of the people had criminal records, some of them had come up NO RECORDS
FOUND. I had gotten about five or six names deep into
the fax when I began to see the pattern. They were all
women.

I started at the beginning again. The first name on
the list was Robin Ray. Mrs. James Vandecourt's first
name was Robin. The tall, cool blonde. The third name
in the stack of criminal record searches was Elise
Barnes. Mrs. Walter Shore's first name was Elise. The
trim little woman with dark hair and the friendly but
slightly timid manner. The fourth name on the list . . .

Then I realized what had happened. When I had given the list of employees to Allgood, I must have had the membership list in my hand, too. He had taken both of them from me, run all the members through the computer. No wonder Martha Herrington was pissed. I went through the stack one more time. As I did, my eyes began to widen.

What in the world was going on here? About half of the members of the lodge seemed to have left no footprints in the criminal justice system. But at least half of the members of the Hellespont Lodge had actually done time in prison—quite a few of them for major offenses. Two of them had even been put away for murder. I felt chilly, like a draft was suddenly coming through the window.

There it was in black and white. Robin Vandecourt had apparently been a prostitute.

Oh, yes, and there was one more puzzling thing. Allgood said that he had run the entire staff and they had come up clean. But that wasn't accurate: this time when he ran them, one name had come up dirty. Raiford Biggs. According to the NCIC, he had been convicted of six offenses; four of them were minor drug offenses, one was for poaching, and two were for aggravated assault.

Seemed like the fox was guarding the henhouse.

CHAPTER 16

WALKED DOWN to my mother's room, banged on the door, but she didn't answer. I was getting hungry and realized that it was time for lunch.

Downstairs in the Grill Room I found all the ladies sitting around in their camo, eating venison burgers off big rough-hewn tables and dabbing at their mouths with heavy linen napkins. Once again I had that icky, sinking, back-in-high-school feeling in the pit of my stomach. Where should I sit? Who should I talk to? What if they think my clothes are funny? What if they don't like me?

As it turned out, the question of where I should sit was answered for me. All of the tables were full except one, which had a sole occupant.

"May I?" I said.

"By all means, honey," the woman said. As soon as I sat, I felt comfortable. Most of the ladies at the lodge had the look of aging debutantes: thin, pretty, trained in all the social graces, maybe a little high-strung. But this woman seemed different. First, she was fat. Some fat people seem uneasy with their fatness and some embrace it. This woman was the latter sort: there was an easiness in her skin that most of the other women at the lodge didn't seem to have. She held out her hand, shook firmly. "Emily Stubbins," she said. "You must be Sunny Childs."

"That's right."

"Heard you saw Moby Dick yesterday. Congratulations. I'd give my right arm to get a crack at that old bastard."

"Well, you know . . ."

She probed my face for a moment with canny green eyes. "I assume you're actually here for the hunting?"

"Sorry?"

She jerked her thumb derisively at the other two tables. "Most of these gals are here for the female bonding. They don't care two farts in a windstorm about hunting." She peered at me for a while. "I mean, nothing personal, but you don't seem to fit in with all the glamour-pusses over there. So—given that there's nothing to do here but hang out with the girls or shoot animals—I'm guessing you're here to hunt."

"You're right," I said. "I am here to hunt."

Emily Stubbins jammed a heaping forkful of field peas and ham hocks in her mouth, then said, "So. What's your story?"

"My story?"

Her eyes crinkled. "Your story. Everybody here has a story. What's yours?"

"I've lived in Atlanta most of my life. Went to college up North. Worked on Wall Street for a couple years. Hated it. Came back. Lived in Atlanta ever since."

She chewed noisily, looking slightly puzzled. "That's it?"

"Is there supposed to be more?"

"Normally, honey, yeah."

I started eating my venison burger. Martha Herring-ton had been right. Uma was a marvelous cook. I've eaten some pretty skanky deer in my time, but this was juicy, tender, not too gamy—but still with a little wild bite to it.

"What about you?" I said. "You have a story?"

"Of course." She grinned. "I'm Mrs. Boyard Stub-bins." She said it in an ironic tone of voice.

I wasn't sure quite how that made a story. Boyard Stubbins was the president of Emory University. Like all of the women here, she was married to an Atlanta worthy. But that didn't add up to a story as far as I was concerned. "Go on," I said.

She shrugged. "Otherwise, pretty much the usual. I was born up in East Tennessee. Didn't even have in-door plumbing. Mama died when I was born, so I was raised by my daddy and four older brothers. Difference between me and them"—she nodded at the women at the next table—"is that after I graduated cum laude from East Tennessee State, I got my Ph.D. from Har-vard, been teaching anthro at Emory for years. No gar-den club, no ladies auxiliary."

I nodded. There was something elliptical about this conversation, as though it rotated around some dark, unseen planet. What I'm saying, I felt sure I was miss-ing something—I just didn't know what it was. But I had a hunch that it had something to do with what I'd found in all those NCIC files that Agent Allgood had sent over.

"This place, I tell you," she said, "would make a hell of an anthropological study."

"You think?"

"Are you not comfortable talking about this?" she said.

"This."

We eyed each other for a while. "You don't know what the hell I'm talking about," she said finally.

"Maybe I don't."

"How'd you become a member here without . . ." Her face clouded for a moment, then she closed her eyes. Then her eyes snapped open. "Son of a bitch!" she said. "It just came to me."

"What did?" '

"You!" A broad grin spread across her face. "I knew your name was familiar from something, but it took me a while. I saw you on TV last year. The thing about Georgia Burnett, that country singer who got killed." She lowered her voice. "You're a private investigator, aren't you?"

I looked around the room furtively. "Okay, yeah, but—"

"My oh my oh my." She gave me a conspiratorial grin and lowered her voice even further, almost to a whisper this time. "You're investigating the Jennifer Treadaway thing, aren't you?"

"Look, I'm just here for the hunting."

"Yeah, right." She laughed, a big booming noise that drew the eyes of all the ladies at the other tables. She smiled broadly at them, with an expression that was just this side of sarcastic, and they all looked away again. Her voice went low again. "Who hired you? Jennifer Treadaway's husband?"

"I'm just here—"

"Yeah, yeah. For the hunting." She stuffed the last

of her venison burger in her mouth, then chewed on it for a while with her mouth half open. "I could help, you know."

"I don't know what to say."

"What I'm curious about, how did you get into the club?"

"My mom's a member. Miranda Wiseberg."

Emily's eyebrows went up. "*You're* Miranda Wiseberg's daughter? Y'all don't favor too much."

"That's a relief."

This drew a big laugh. "She's a legend here, of course."

"Oh? She doesn't seem to come down here very often. Hell, I don't think she even *pretends* to enjoy hunting."

Emily frowned at me. "Okay, okay, that's it, you're definitely here undercover. Somehow, you're undercover."

"Why do you say that?"

She looked at me with her bright, canny eyes. "Because it's obvious to me that you don't understand the first thing about the Hellespont Lodge is."

"It's a hunting lodge for rich ladies," I said.

"It *appears* to be a hunting lodge for rich ladies. If you were really being inducted as a member, you'd know that's just a front."

I felt like some sort of realization was slowly, slowly crystallizing in my slow little brain. "A front."

Her big voice went down to a whisper again. "Sunny, to become a member of the Hellespont Lodge, you must be a gold digger. Every woman here was born poor, married a rich man, moved up, let's say, substantially, on the social food chain. And ideally, you have to be passing yourself off as a somebody who's had money in the family for generations."

My jaw must have dropped. But boy, it sure explained a lot of things, didn't it? All those criminal records, for one thing.

"That's why your mama's a legend, Sunny: she married—what?—*three* rich guys?"

"My father, she married for love," I said. "Dr. Wiseberg, her current husband, is rich guy number four."

Emily spread her large hands. "There. See?" She studied my face curiously. "Okay. Further deduction from facts in evidence: if you didn't know all of this, then somebody inside the organization snuck you in without telling you the truth about the lodge." She looked over at the next table. "If I were to bet, I'd put my money on Martha Herrington."

"Do you ever get tired of teaching anthropology to snotty seventeen-year-olds?" I said.

"Why?"

"Because I would love to hire you. You'd make a hell of an investigator."

Her moon of a face brightened, and then she came out with her big booming laugh.

"Let's just say you're right," I said. "For the sake of argument. Tell me what you know about Jennifer Treadaway."

"I'm not exactly part of the In Crowd here." She frowned. "But even someone of my substantial social deficiencies could see that she was pretty well hated here."

"How so?"

"You know how these people are. Smiling and hugging and kissy-kissy. That's on the outside. But you peel back the skin and it's one cat fight after another around here. Takes a lot of reading the tea leaves, though, to figure out when the smiling and the kissy-kissy means they hate you, and when it means they love you."

"That is precisely the reason I left the South when I went off to college. I never could figure out how to be a good Southern woman."

"And yet you came back."

"Love-hate relationship, I guess." I shrugged. "So anyway, trained anthropologist that you are, you read the huggy-kissy stuff and determined that Jennifer Treadaway was not well liked."

This drew a smile. A piece of deer burger was lodged in Emily Stubbins's teeth. "Drinks are served here at five o'clock on the nose. The key to learning about the ladies around here is to wait till they get drunk. That's when you see the real deal." Her voice went low. "Would you believe I saw cute little Mrs. Walter Shore over there rolling around on the floor with Jennifer one time? Slapping and scratching and pulling hair? Looked like something off Jerry Springer."

I snuck a glance over at the next table. Pert, smiling little Mrs. Walter Shore. It was hard to believe.

"And Robin Vandecourt? She got liquored up one time, pulled a little old chrome-plated .25 automatic on somebody. They had to call Horst. He knocked her down and tied her to a chair with a piece of rope. She must have hollered for two hours. Gonna kill everybody, gonna kick everybody's ass, F this, F that. I had four brothers, man, I *never* heard language like that."

I tried to imagine the tall cool woman spouting death threats while trussed like a hog. It kind of threw things in a different light.

"Next morning," Emily Stubbins continued, "everybody's kissy-kissy again."

"Okay," I said, "but can you think of anybody with a specific motive for wanting Jennifer dead?"

"Specific? Not really."

"Why did everybody dislike her?"

Emily Stubbins frowned. "I honestly don't know. I'll tell you this, though: she tried to bum some money from me one time. And when I said no, she got . . . let's say she got insistent."

"Meaning what?"

"Oh, vague threats about how she was going to reveal my obscure origins to the cream of Atlanta society."

"What did you tell her?"

"Quote, I'm proud to be a fat, crazy old redneck and I don't give a flying foo-foo who knows it, unquote. That shut her up."

"Foo-foo?" I said.

"It might have been another word." She winked at me, then stood up with her plate in hand. "Now, I have flat *got* my eye on that bread pudding over there."

CHAPTER 17

"CAN I HAVE a word, Mom?" I said when my mother walked into the Grill Room.

She must have seen something on my face. "All that pent-up anger will give you wrinkles, you know," she said.

"I'm serious," I said. "I need to talk."

She smiled at me, eyes wide, waiting.

"Get your food," I said. Then I went and sat down.

"You've always been such a peremptory person," she said in her sweetest voice as she sat down with her salad. "There are much better ways, you know."

"Why didn't you tell me?" I said.

"Tell you?"

"About this group." I kept my voice low. There were still a couple of women sitting at one of the other tables. "How come you never told me this was a club for gold diggers? How come you never told me that all these women were just a bunch of grasping, mean-spirited social climbers who would eat their young for a dollar? It might have made my investigation run a lot smoother."

"*All* these women?" she said quietly.

"That's the membership qualification, isn't it? Start poor, claw your way up out of the working class by screwing rich men?"

"You include me in that sweeping statement, of course." She kept smiling. Then she stabbed a piece of tomato, ate it slowly. Her eyes, twinkling away, didn't leave my face until she was done eating her salad.

"Let me see if I understand what you're implying," she said when she was done. "The members of the lodge have come up in the world, in part through the use of feminine charms and so on, and therefore, what, anyone in the club is capable of murder? Something like that?"

"I didn't say that. But I ran an NCIC on all these people and guess what came up? Prostitution, manslaughter, aggravated assault, DUI, pandering, solicitation, possession with intent, you name it."

My mother's little smile hung there on her face. "Come with me," she said finally. Her voice was very quiet. Which is always a bad sign. It means I've really offended her, really pissed her off.

"What?" I said.

She patted her mouth delicately with her linen napkin, then stood. "Indulge me, sweetheart."

I sighed loudly, just like I did back when I was fourteen. I may have rolled my eyes, too. But I followed her. Down the hallway, out the side door, over to the parking area full of Lincoln Navigators and Range Rovers and Cadillacs. She got into the driver's side of her Cadillac, so I sat down next to her.

And off we went, down the gravel drive, out the entrance, onto the county road heading back toward Hightower.

"What?" I said again.

My mother has always been a lead foot driver. But this was ridiculous. Picture, if you will, a sixty-year-old woman wearing head-to-toe camouflage, her dyed red hair pulled back in a ponytail, hard-knuckled hands gripping both sides of the wheel, driving like Richard Petty. It's not a pretty sight. The tires of the big Caddy screeched and complained on every turn as Mom powered the massive car through the pine forests of Williams County. I just held on for dear life: there's no getting in Mom's way when she's like this.

She didn't speak and neither did I as we swept past the occasional decrepit mobile home, each bare patch of ground scattered with sleeping yard-dogs and rusting cars, through the middle of the miserable little town of Hightower, through more unbroken pine forests, and then onto the interstate. She headed south toward Columbus on the Alabama border, the speedometer registering just over 90.

Then we were off onto another state road heading through peanut country, the area down around where Jimmy Carter grew up.

"Mom . . ." I said.

But she just kept rolling, heedless of cops or curves or the 35-mile-an-hour speed limits in the occasional dusty towns through which we roared. The land had flattened out here, and long bare fields of beans and peanuts stretched out to the horizons.

We had been driving for about forty-five minutes since we left the lodge, and my mother had not spoken a word. We turned from the state road onto a county road and then from a county road onto a winding little track that was barely more than a tractor path. The peanut fields whizzed by. I was beginning to grow intensely curious about the purpose of this whirlwind tour. But I was damned if I was going to ask.

"Oh!" Mom said suddenly, as though something had taken her by surprise.

To our left another tiny road appeared. Mom slammed on her brakes, spun the wheel, and we drifted sideways, the tires shrieking. It seemed to take a long time. But finally we had stopped, the Caddy coming to rest on the side of the road facing dead into the middle of a peanut field. To my right was a small hill overrun with kudzu. Underneath the kudzu was an unidentifiable lump about ten or fifteen feet high.

My mother got out of the car and began picking her way through the kudzu. I followed her. Eventually we reached the lump—which I was now able to make out as being a ruined wooden shed or shack. My mother pulled some kudzu off the shack, revealing a decrepit porch. A chimney of rocks and mismatched brick had toppled over to the side of the little shed.

"Okay," I said.

My mother was looking at the shack with an unreadable expression on her face, her eyes distant.

"Here it is, little baby," she said. "You've always made such sport of my obscure origins. Well, now you know." She pointed into the kudzu. "This is where I was born. Right there in the back room. My mother died here giving birth to my little sister. My father was a tenant of the man who owned that house." She pointed to a large, plain farmhouse, way off on the other side of the vast peanut field.

"This is the place where I spent the first fifteen years of my life. I never had a new pair of shoes or a new dress or a piece of steak in all those fifteen years. We were the family that poor folks at some little Pentecostal church would get together at Christmas and buy a canned ham for, some Saltines, a couple cans of cranberry sauce. Maybe give us a hand-me-down wagon, or a cornshuck doll. Even poor kids around here got the small luxury of laughing at me and my sister and my father, calling us white trash, shell pickers, white niggers."

She gave a grand sweep of her hand. "This is the place, little baby. This is the place where we used to chip ice off the seat of the outhouse so we could go to the bathroom at night. This is the place where my father came down with TB, and where the only doctor in town wouldn't treat him because Daddy couldn't pay cash for his services. This is the place where my father hung around coughing and hacking until he died. This is the place where I was fourteen years old, trying to take care of my baby sister, and my older brother— who was slow in the head, as they used to say—with no father, no mother, no money, no nothing.

"This is the place where the man who lived over there"—she pointed again at the distant farmhouse, "used to come and 'comfort' me in my time of need."

With her foot, she tested the tread of the warped step leading up to what had been the porch of the shack. When it didn't crumble, she sat down on it. I sat down next to her.

She looked across the field at the distant farmhouse, with no expression in her eyes. "You've always been a judgmental girl," Mom said. "That's not all bad. It's part of what gives you your edge. But what I'm saying is, until you've walked a mile in the shoes of all those

girls over at the lodge, till you've seen the trailer parks
and flophouses they grew up in, the parents who aban-
doned them, the men who beat them, the kids who spit
on them, the pitiful clothes they wore, the cold that
blew through the walls of their houses—until you've
seen all of that, don't begrudge them a little comfort,
a little stability, a little predictability in their lives. And
don't assume you understand them."

We sat for a long time. It was a beautiful day, quiet,
cool, the air feeling clean and crisp, the blue sky over
us full of fluffy picture book clouds.

"Let me ask you something," my mother said. "And
I want you to understand that I'm not saying this to
make you feel bad. I'm asking you an honest question.
If you really believe that it's so terrible to choose
money over love, then why are you here, my dear?
Why are you working to make a few trifling dollars
when you could be lying on some sunny beach down
in the Caribbean next to the man you're always insist-
ing to me that you love? Hm? Why is that?"

"Mommy, Mommy," I said, "I'm so sorry." Then I
started to cry. She held me in her fierce grip for a long
time.

"Long time ago, I gave up being sorry about anything I ever done. Ain't no point in being sorry, little
girl."

I couldn't remember hearing my mother say "ain't"
before, not once in my life.

Afterward, as we were driving back to the lodge, this
time at a more sedate pace, I said, "What was his
name?"

"Who?"

"The asshole. The farmer."

"My father was a lovely man, but useless. If he'd stayed alive, I imagine I'd be married to some dumb peanut farmer, slowly going bankrupt on three hundred acres of mediocre land."

"What was his *name*?" I said again.

"That asshole, when it was all over and done with, he sent me off to Agnes Scott College, paid the full freight, so I could go up there to Atlanta and learn how people lived who weren't in debt all their lives, who could afford doctors when they were sick, who didn't have to grind themselves to powder working in fields or turning the same screw day after day in some factory. That asshole changed my life." She said this in a neutral voice. Then, after a moment: "His name was Leon Aldridge."

"And you really don't resent what he did? Honest to God?"

She didn't answer this immediately. But once we'd gotten back onto the interstate, I noticed she was smiling just a tiny bit.

"What?" I said.

"About ten years ago, Leon Aldridge, Jr.—his son— got into some financial trouble. I bought up his entire farm. He pays me rent now, and every now and then, when peanut prices are low, I have to go down there and read him the riot act while he bows and scrapes and whimpers." She raised her eyebrows slightly. "Not that this gives me pleasure or anything."

We both laughed for a while. My mom. You gotta love her.

CHAPTER 18

WHEN WE GOT back to the lodge, I tracked down Martha Herrington. "Look," I said, "an emergency has come up and I really can't finish this engagement. I'll have my bookkeeper return your check."

Then I turned and walked out of the lodge.

As I drove away, I glanced in the rearview mirror and saw Biggs, the gamekeeper's assistant, staring after me with his strange black eyes.

Twenty-four hours later I walked onto a beach in a small resort on the island of Barbados. I was wearing a one piece and flip-flops, carrying a towel and some lotion.

I found Barrington lying on a wooden lounge chair under a huge beach umbrella, wearing baggy yellow swim trunks and sunglasses, reading a book called *Field Manual of Wiretapping*. Only the toes of his left foot were peeping out in the sun. He had admitted to me once, after several scotches, that he was a little vain about the lightness of his mocha-colored skin, that he didn't like getting it dark from exposure to the sun. *You wouldn't understand,* he had said, with an odd smile. *It's a black thing.*

I had to stand there a long time before he looked up. With the sunglasses on, I couldn't get any read on what he was thinking when he finally looked up at me.

"Watch out," I said. "Your toes are getting awful brown."

He closed the book, set it over his groin, still looking at me through his sunglasses.

"Look," I said, "I made a mistake."

Still no read from his face.

"So, hey," I said, shifting back and forth. "Do you want to get married?"

He didn't say anything for a while. "To whom?" he said finally.

"Ha ha."

I kept standing there.

"No, Barrington, I'm serious. Will you marry me?"

He took a long breath. "Sunny? It's not that easy. You can't fix it that way."

Then he stood, put his towel around his shoulders, slipped his feet into a pair of braided leather slippers, and started walking away from me across the sand, tiny arcs of sand drifting through the air behind his feet.

CHAPTER 19

I GOT BACK to Atlanta just in time to lead my regular Tuesday night women's self-defense class. I drove the women way too hard and one new student ended up walking out in tears. I didn't seem to be helping her much on the self-empowerment front. Then I went home and drank cheap red wine and listened to the Stanley Brothers sing songs about lost love and death until things began spinning. After that, I don't remember much.

The phone started ringing at about four in the morning. I let it ring. It rang again five minutes later. Then again. Then again. Then my cell started going off. Finally I'd had enough, so I picked up the receiver.

"What!" I shouted.

"It's Mom."

"And?"

There was a long pause. "It happened again."

"What did?"

"Martha Herrington. She's dead. I think we need you down here."

CHAPTER 20

I GOT THERE at about the same time that Sheriff Timmers and his medical assistant, Rochelle Longineau, drove up in a big black Lincoln with a gold star on the side. Through the trees I could see the body, covered by a sheet, lying on the ground beneath one of the many tree stands on the lodge's property. A number of dumb-looking sheriff's deputies were milling around near it, kicking leaves and trampling on evidence. A couple more stood up in the tree stand, one of them dribbling tobacco juice over the side onto the ground. Twelve or fifteen women wearing camouflage outfits stood in a semicircle, talking somberly, their faces ashen. If this was a crime scene, it was rapidly being contaminated.

Rochelle left the old man in the Lincoln, and walked quickly toward the sheet. I followed her.

"What you fools think you're doing?" she said to one deputy, a large white boy who was sitting on a stump five feet from the body, carving his name in the wood with a jackknife.

"Do what?" he said blankly.

"Where's the crime scene tape?" She was clearly

exasperated. "Huh? Get these people back. And how come you bunch of nitwits are trampling all over everything? Didn't I tell you on the radio not to touch anything?"

One of the deputies said, "Yeah, but the sherf, he done said—"

"I don't care *what* he said! Y'all get the hell away from the body. Ladies! Get back. Deputy Martin, string some crime scene tape. Y'all two, get your fool selves out of that tree stand!"

"Shoot, Nurse," the big deputy said, "it ain't nothing but a hunting accident. This lady done fell out the tree, cut herself open on a limb coming down."

"That may be. But the only way we can determine that is if we conduct a proper examination."

She then walked toward the white sheet. I followed. As soon as she pulled back the sheet, I knew it was no hunting accident.

"Entry wound under the left ear," I said. "Same as Jennifer Treadaway."

Rochelle nodded, her black skin practically radiating anger. "These idiots," she said. "Look at what these morons did." She pointed at an array of footprints in the soft dirt around the victim. Then she glanced at my own feet. "You aren't helping anything, sister. Step back, please."

I ignored her, picked up the other side of the sheet. Under the sheet I found two bare feet sticking out of the cuffs of a pair of camouflage pants. Even from where I was standing, I could smell bleach. "The maids already get out here to wash her feet?" I said.

"Behind the tape, Miss Childs," Rochelle Longineau said. "Behind the tape."

I dropped the sheet and retreated across a mat of pine needles so as not to leave any footprints.

Rochelle Longineau was striding through the woods toward the huddled little man in the wheelchair. "Sheriff. Sheriff. You need to get on the horn right now, call the GBI."

"Hooo *hoooooooo!*" the sheriff said. "Look at all them folks. One of them rich gals must of bagged 'em a ten-pointer."

"All I've got to say, Rochelle," I said, "is the sooner you run for sheriff, the better for the people of Williams County."

Half an hour later I was standing next to my mother in the big meeting room at the lodge, all the members assembled in front of us. Several were still crying, and everyone was visibly shaken.

"Ladies," my mother declaimed, "I know most of you have already met my daughter, Sunny. It's time to get some things out in the open. Sunny is a private investigator. She was hired by the lodge at Martha Herrington's directive to investigate the unfortunate incident that happened last year. Her membership in the club was only a ruse. Some of you may find it rather shocking that Martha Herrington, with no direct sanction from the board of directors, installed a private investigator here. I find it a little shocking myself. I am consoled, however, in the fact that, by complete accident, the investigator Martha hired turned out to be my daughter.

"Now, ladies, we find ourselves today in uncharted waters. Under any other circumstances, I would ask Sunny to leave right this minute. However, given that she is my daughter and, therefore, someone whom I believe the membership can trust, it is my contention that we ought to continue to employ her services.

"Why? First, of course, because justice needs to be done here. Not that I don't trust the GBI, but . . ." She shrugged broadly. "But perhaps of equal importance, this lodge is about to undergo the sort of scrutiny that no one in our circle can possibly relish. The sooner we find out who that killer is, the sooner the spotlight will move elsewhere. I don't think I have to spell out what I'm talking about here."

There was a brief murmur. Finally Robin Vande-court spoke. "Of course I'm not speaking personally to you, Miranda—or to your lovely and no doubt talented daughter. But I *must* say I find it terribly offensive that someone came into our midst telling us a lie about who she was and why she was here. It makes me feel a little dirty."

"If I can respond to that?" I said.

"I'd rather you not," my mother said. "Now, Robin, honey, you and I both know that the lives of virtually everyone in this room have involved a certain amount of, shall we say . . . subterfuge? Let's take you for an example. There are quite a few women in our circle who might feel somewhat—to use your words—*dirty*, if they knew that all those amusing stories about your years at Sweetbriar were not entirely accurate. As I recall, most of your late adolescence was, in fact, spent doing something considerably less genteel than attend-ing an all-girl college in Virginia. Something involving men sticking dollar bills in your G-string, maybe? So let's all be careful about being the pot that calls the kettle black."

Robin Vandecourt's lovely face stiffened.

"God knows, I don't say that to cause you embarrassment, honey," Mom continued. "We all have our pasts, myself included. As for Martha's decision to hire my daughter—particularly the fact that she did it without consulting anyone—well, I'm not entirely comfortable with that either. But the decision can't be undone. And given that we find ourselves in our current uncomfortable fix, let us be realists, ladies. My daughter is a professional. This is what she does. The sooner we can find out what happened here, the more we can control the situation. The more we control the situation, the fewer potentially embarrassing revelations about all of us."

"Well, you can do whatever you want," Robin Vandecourt said. "But I'm going home."

My mother smiled brightly. "Oh, no, dear, you aren't. Neither are any of the rest of you. We're all just going to perch right here for a few days and together we're going to sort this thing out. Just like a big, happy family."

Robin Vandecourt's smile was frosty. "Sweetheart, I really don't see how you're going to keep me here."

Mom batted her eyes. "Unless you want your husband's friends asking you to do table dances at the next cotillion ball, I suggest you stay. Am I being sufficiently plain?"

Robin Vandecourt locked eyes with my mother and they smiled back and forth for several seconds. "Miranda," she finally said to my mother, "you are not an entirely nice person."

"Never said I was, darling." Mom looked around the room, her green eyes steely. "The GBI will have an agent here shortly. I expect that you all will make time to speak with Sunny prior to his arrival. I think I speak for all of us when I say we don't want any surprises coming out. Sunny? Anything you'd like to say at this point?"

"Yes," I said. "First, folks, I apologize for any abuse I may have made of your trust. I hope you'll appreciate that I was only doing my job. Now, on to more pressing issues. Who found Martha Herrington?"

"I think it was Biggs," Mrs. Walter Shore said.

"And whom did he notify?"

"Me," my mother said.

"And who went out to where she fell?"

Almost everyone's hands went up.

"Were any of you alone with her at any point?"

"Me," my mother said.

"Anyone else?"

No one moved.

"One last thing. Given that the killer is still at large, I'd like to bring down several of my operatives from Atlanta to act as security."

"Everybody comfortable with that?" Mom said.

Nods from all the women in the room.

"All right," I said, "I'm going to interview my mother first. Everyone else, I'd like you to return to your rooms. Don't talk to each other, don't compare notes. And folks? Somebody around here has already killed two of you, so lock your doors."

After the ladies had trooped upstairs to their rooms, I sat down with my mother.

"Well?" I said.

Her face was a mask of self-control. She waited until

the last of the women had left the room, then she began weeping. I tried to give her a hug but she pushed me gently away. "I'm fine," she said, dabbing at her eyes. As per the regulations of the lodge, she wasn't wearing makeup—or if she was, it wasn't visible. Despite her various face-lifts and tucks, her age was showing in the tiny crow's feet around the eyes, the sag of tissue in the hollows of the cheek.

"I've never seen anything like that before," she said.

"How exactly did you find out Martha was dead?"

"I was in my room. I'd gone out to sit around in my tree stand—but as you know, I don't really care for hunting. I guess I'm just here for the camaraderie. Anyway, I was bored silly sitting out there, so I came back early. I had just sat down to read a book when Biggs burst in the door."

"What exactly did he say to you?"

She looked thoughtful. "He said, 'I'm afraid it's happened again, Mrs. Wiseberg.' I said, 'Who?' and he said, 'Mrs. Herrington.' "

"And then?"

"I called Horst and asked him to notify the sheriff's office, then I took a sheet from the laundry room, and Biggs drove me out to where she was lying."

"Was anybody else there?"

"No."

"Any sign that anything had been disturbed?"

Mom looked slightly irritated. "I'm not Natty Bumpo. How would I know if anything had been disturbed?"

I sighed. "I have no idea."

Mom took a deep breath. "I didn't like Martha Herrington terribly much. But this . . ."

"Let's talk about that. Can you think of anybody who might have had reason to kill her?"

"Don't be ridiculous."

"I'm not being ridiculous. Obviously *somebody* had reason to do this thing."

Mom was silent.

"Mom, before I left, I got the impression that Jennifer Treadaway had made some feeble attempts—I don't know if you'd call it blackmail or not—but she hit up several members here for money, while making vague implications that she would betray their secrets if they didn't pay up. Is there any possible connection to Martha here?"

Mom didn't answer.

"Mom? Is it possible that Jennifer and Martha were involved in something like that together? Some kind of blackmail scheme?"

"Jennifer approached me the same way. But I never heard a peep from Martha along those lines."

"Were they close friends?"

"Not really."

"So it doesn't seem likely to you that there's a blackmail connection."

My mother shook her head.

"Okay, let's turn to what you saw today. Did you see Martha Herrington this morning?"

"Yes. She was at breakfast around five. Then we got on the little golf cart tram that Biggs uses to drive the girls around to their stands in."

"How many of you were on the tram?"

Mom closed her eyes. "It was me, Bonnie Hathaway, Elise Shore, Robin Vandecourt, Rose Ellen Knight, and Martha."

I jotted down the names. "And what order were they taken to their tree stands?"

"I don't know. Biggs dropped me off first."

"And what time was this?"

"Around quarter till six. Just before sunrise."

"One last thing. When you found Martha, was she wearing her boots?"

Mom shook her head. "No, she wasn't. She was barefoot." She looked off into the distance. "It's the strangest thing. When I found her, I thought I smelled something, something quite incongruous. Though I can't really place what it was."

"Bleach?"

Mom's eyes widened. "Why yes! That's it exactly. How in the world did you know?"

CHAPTER 21

I WALKED UPSTAIRS and knocked on the door labeled MRS. WALTER SHORE. The lodge wasn't like a hotel: every member had a permanent room where they could keep their things throughout the year.

"Who is it?" a tremulous voice answered.

"It's Sunny."

The door opened a crack, then Elise Shore peered out. After she'd confirmed who I was, she opened the door and said, "Come in, darling, come in."

I walked in and sat on a couch upholstered in red and orange silk.

"Isn't this just the most awful thing?" she said. "I just can't stop crying."

"I know how you feel."

She peered at me intently. "You and your mother are just such *strong* people. I envy that. I'm just as weak as a dishrag. Always have been."

She was a pretty, delicate-featured woman of about fifty, with an even smaller stature than my own. There was an eagerness to please and a softness about her that belied what I knew about her past.

"My lord, I've just never seen anything like this in my life, Sunny!"

"Oh really?"

She blinked, cocked her head slightly. "Gracious, I'm sure you don't mean to sound that way, but your tone of voice is so . . . accusatory."

"Maybe I did mean it to sound that way."

Her birdlike eyes studied me nervously. "Are you trying to suggest I had something to do with . . . this? With what happened to poor Martha?"

"Last week I ran criminal histories on the membership of the lodge. It turned up some fascinating information."

Mrs. Walter Shore's face went white.

"When you say you're weak as a dishrag," I said, "you don't mean that in the sense that you're a person who's entirely incapable of taking vigorous action when the need arises."

She closed her eyes and slumped back in her richly upholstered chair.

"Well?" I said.

"That has *nothing* to do with this."

"You want to tell me about it?"

"What I'll tell you is this. I went out this morning in the same tram as Martha. I was the second person dropped off. I got up in my tree stand and I sat there all morning. When I got back, they said she was dead. I was not Martha's greatest fan, I will be the first to admit. But did I murder her? That's laughable."

"Why is it laughable? I've seen your sheet."

She covered her face with her hands and her shoulders quaked for a while. Finally she said, "My father died when I was eight. My mother had emotional difficulties. I grew up living in motels and trailer courts and bus terminals and occasionally in cars and under bridges. When I was fourteen, a man showed me some attention. He was forty-six years old, but I thought he would save me from the uncertainties of my life. We were married the following year, two days after I turned fifteen. He then took me to a house out in the country that he had just inherited—along with about sixty thousand dollars—from his mother. He then proceeded to drink and play cards for a year and a half, while he spent all the money he had inherited. Meantime, he wouldn't allow me to leave the house. He wouldn't allow me to have friends. He told me what to wear, how to cut my hair, what to eat, when to stand up, and when to sit down. On one occasion I had a three-sentence conversation with one of his card-playing buddies. For that grotesque display of disloyalty (those are the very words he used), he beat me so badly I spent a month and a half in the hospital.

"When I was sixteen, I got pregnant. Apparently this didn't suit him. He was running low on money and he said that a child would be too expensive. When my little girl was born, he took her by the ankle, carried her out into the yard, and threw her forty feet up into a tree. She hung up there on a branch in that old live oak tree, crying and crying and crying for twelve hours before she died. After she finally slipped away, he got drunk and fell asleep in bed. There I was, twelve hours after giving birth, so you can imagine how I felt. But notwithstanding that, I went out and climbed up that tree, and took my little girl down and buried her in the yard. That was the only strong thing I've ever done in my life. Then I went back inside, poured my husband's whiskey all over the floor, and I set it on fire. It was my intention to burn myself to death. But when the fire started getting hot, I just couldn't stand it. I was too weak to stay. And so I ran out of the house. Then I sat there on my daughter's grave and watched the house burn down and kill my husband."

We sat for a while in silence.

"So, Sunny, I wouldn't presume, if I were you, to know what I am or am not capable of, just because of what's written on some piece of paper down in some courthouse. Did I serve three years in jail for manslaughter? Yes, I did. If I were in that situation again, would I do it the same way? Perhaps. But if I heard you correctly while I was standing around near poor Martha's body this morning, you said that Martha was knifed. Martha was a large, vigorous woman. So even if I were capable of such a horrendous act—and I believe that I am not—the likelihood of a little bitty thing like me successfully killing a big strapping woman like Martha? As I say—laughable."

Mrs. Walter Shore's hands were trembling.

"Okay," I said. "Let's back up. What did you see this morning?"

"Nothing. We rode the tram out, I got off, the tram kept going. That's all. Next thing I knew, she was dead."

"When I spoke to y'all last week, you implied that Jennifer Treadaway was blackmailing people here at the lodge. Any possibility that Martha was involved with that?"

"Dale Herrington the Fourth, Martha's husband, is one of the wealthiest men in Atlanta. It's inconceivable that she would have motivation to blackmail anybody."

"Jennifer Treadaway's husband was not exactly poor."

"Mr. Treadaway is a real estate developer. Those people are all boom and bust. He went through a bust cycle and Jennifer got a little desperate. But he simply isn't in the same league as Dale Herrington. Mr. Herrington's money is very old and very stable. Financial motive? No, simply doesn't make sense."

"She never approached you for money?"

"Oh my gracious no!"

"Then what connects Jennifer and Martha? Why would somebody do this?"

"I'm sure it was a sex pervert. Probably one of the colored men that work around here or that creepy Biggs person."

"Jennifer Treadaway, so far as the ME could tell, wasn't sexually molested in any way."

"Maybe he just didn't get the chance. Maybe she resisted and he panicked."

"That's possible," I said. "But I still think there's some kind of connection."

"Well, I can't think what it would be. Neither of them liked each other in the slightest."

I knocked on Rose Ellen Knight's door next. "So you're a private investigator, huh?" she said, ushering me in. Her television was blaring. She was wearing workout clothes that showed off every curve of her body. She was younger than most of the women at the lodge and seemed to enjoy showing off her assets. "I should have known. You didn't seem like you fit in."

"How so?"

She squinted at me, looking me up and down. "I don't mean you're ugly or whatever, but you don't give the impression of being somebody who gives men what they want."

"What do they want?"

She sucked in her gut, stuck out her silicone boobs, rolled her eyes back, and opened her mouth languidly. "Oh, God, baby, you're so goooooood!" she moaned. "You're so biiiiiig!" Then she laughed, a loud, coarse cackle. "You know—*that*."

"No," I said. "Whatever *that* is, it's never been my strong suit."

"You'll never get paid if you can't do that." She looked me up and down again, then poked my left breast with a long fingernail. "I could recommend a good doctor to do something about those, too."

"No thanks," I said drily.

"Suit yourself." She flopped down on her couch, threw one long leg over the arm, turned off the TV with the remote control, then tossed the remote on the coffee table, where it landed next to a very large vibrator. "So old Martha bit the big one today, huh?"

"Gee, please contain your grief," I said.

She laughed her coarse laugh again. "Martha Herrington was an asshole. I'm not sorry she's dead."

"That seems a little harsh."

"Hey, babe, just being honest. I had a good conversation with your mama one time. She told me, 'Honey, never look back.' That was great advice. Martha's dead, what a shame, but I'm not gonna lay around boo-hooing about it."

"You were on the tram with her this morning."

"Yeah."

"Who was with her when you got dropped off at your stand?"

"Biggs dropped the other girls off, then me. At that point, it was just Martha in the tram and Biggs driving the golf cart."

"You think Biggs did it?"

"He is an icky little shit, isn't he?"

"So that's a yes?"

"Maybe. You think they got killed by the same person?"

"Problem is," I said, "according to Allgood's investigation last year, he had an alibi."

"So that leaves Horst, Uma, their assistants, and a bunch of old rich ladies."

"What do you think about Horst?"

"I had a little sport hump with Horst one time. He's a scary bastard. Made me wear white makeup over my whole body, then lie there like I was dead. It was kind of a kick."

"So what would be his motive?"

"Some kind of sex thing, I guess. Like I say, he seems to like having sex with women who act like they're dead. Why not take it to the next level?"

"There's no evidence of that. At least there wasn't with Jennifer."

"Sunny, I got news for you. It's all about sex. Even when it's not."

"What about you? You have any reason to want either of them dead?"

"There's only one person in the world I want dead."

"Who's that?"

She laughed loudly. "My husband."

"Jesus," I said.

"Look, he's not the worst guy in the world. But he's seventy-eight years old! I mean it gets to be a drag."

She pulled down the straps of her leotard, baring her large, perky breasts and her hard, tanned stomach. "Look at this. It's a goddamn work of art. And I'm giving it away to a seventy-eight-year-old guy who has to wear diapers when he goes out to the grocery store. Doesn't that seem unfair to you?"

"How much money do you get when he dies?"

She shrugged. "Six, eight million."

"Then you just answered your own question."

The big, coarse laugh again. "You are one funny chick. I like you. You're so real."

I got up and headed for the door.

"Hey, Sunny?"

I opened the door. "Yes?"

"You don't go for the girl-girl thing do you?"

"Nope."

She grinned at me, winked, then snapped the straps of her leotard back over her shoulders.

"Too bad. Gets so *boring* around here."

CHAPTER 22

AFTER THAT I talked to the other women who'd been on the tram that morning, but nothing they said was particularly enlightening. None of them could think of anybody with a motive to kill Martha Herrington, none of them had been alone with her, and all of them claimed to have been in their hunting stands most of the morning.

After I was done, I went out and found Biggs in the gun room behind the lodge. Inside the room were rows and rows of rifles and shotguns, secured behind thick glass. He was cleaning a rifle.

"Oh, great," Biggs said when I walked in. "You again."

"I thought you were supposed to be all deferential and humble around the membership," I said.

He fixed his black eyes on me. "You're not a member. You're a snoop."

"I'm a *professional* snoop," I said. "Hired by your employer. So I'd appreciate a little less attitude."

"Legally speaking, I'm not obliged to talk to you." He looked back down at the rifle, ran a patch through the bore with a brass rod.

"You one of these jailhouse lawyers?" I said.

His eyes narrowed. "What's that supposed to mean?"

"I ran you through the FBI computer. Apparently the lodge doesn't do real thorough background checks. Possession with intent. Aggravated assault. I especially like the poaching thing. If I point this out to the membership, I'd say your days of employment here are numbered."

Biggs smiled thinly. "Youthful indiscretions. I'm a bona fide solid citizen now."

"I'm deeply comforted by that. But I doubt all those ladies up there would be."

He lifted the rifle he was cleaning, sighted through the scope at my head.

"And don't ever point a gun at me again," I said.

"Shoot, doll, it ain't loaded."

His finger was resting on the side of the rifle just above the trigger. I walked over and tried to yank his finger backward, but he jerked his hand away. "Now's the part where you confront me with the damning evidence, right, Sunny?" he said. "Huh? 'So, Biggs, it looks bad for you. You were the last person to see the victim alive. Care to explain?' "

"Go ahead," I said. "Answer your own question."

"I drove a bunch of members out to their stands this morning. The last person I delivered was Martha Herrington. She got out of the tram, I shined a flashlight on the ladder so she could climb up the stand. When she was done, I drove off, she was alive. Period."

"You get along okay with Martha Herrington?"

"Never had any problems with her, no."

"Was she wearing boots when she climbed up the ladder?"

"Yep."

"Any idea who could have done this?"

"Yep."

I raised my eyebrows. "Really. Who?"

"Figure it out yourself."

"Why don't you stop playing games."

"No, seriously. You asked who could have done this. I'm saying: who, physically, could have done this? You tell me."

"Probably a man," I said. "Martha Herrington is a fairly large woman. Unless they took her completely by surprise, I doubt the average woman would have the physical strength to pull this off."

"Exactly."

"Which means you, Horst, or one of his helpers."

"You can rule out the helpers. Doggett and Alf, they was both up in Troup County getting the tractor back from the John Deere dealer. That leaves me and Horst."

"You're saying you think Horst did it?"

"I was with Horst all morning. Horst was with me all morning. I'm his alibi and he's mine." He smiled, showing a row of crooked teeth. "Then again, what if we're *both* lying?"

I studied his face. He was giving up nothing.

"You wear a knife all the time, don't you?"

He shrugged. "My job is to clean game. Of course I wear a knife."

"You mind if I see it?"

He pulled his hunting knife out of its sheath, handed it to me. "Tell me about it."

"It's a custom knife made by a guy from Arkansas

named Bob Dozier," he said. "Bought it at the Blade Show in Atlanta last year. Made of D2 steel with a black handle made from a phenolic resin material called Micarta. He calls that model the Elk Hunter. I park it in a cross-draw sheath made of a molded black plastic called Kydex. Hell of a knife."

From the wear pattern on the blade, it was obvious that the five-inch blade had been resharpened many times. I checked the edge with my thumb.

"Sharp enough to shave hair off my arm," Biggs said. "You want to see?"

"Not even hardly." I handed the knife back.

Biggs sheathed the knife. "If I was investigating this thing," he said, "which of course I'm not—I'd forget about suspects and motives. Me, I'd concentrate on the feet. Jennifer Treadaway and Martha Herrington both ended up barefoot, their skin all scrubbed down with bleach. That's a pretty darn unique clue, to my untrained investigative eye. Seems like it would be an important avenue of investigation, huh?" His voice was sarcastic. "Of course, I'm just some dumb ex-con who drives a golf cart around in the woods for a living."

"If I didn't know better, I'd think you were actually trying to help me," I said.

"If I was really trying to help, I'd tell you let the professionals investigate. I'd tell you to stop wasting these ladies' money, head on up to Atlanta, and get back to investigating whiplash cases," he said. "But of course you wouldn't listen to me, so I ain't gonna waste my breath."

He rubbed a cloth down the beautiful wooden stock of the gun he'd been cleaning, put it back in its case, then walked out of the room.

• • •

I found Horst in the office doing paperwork.

"Biggs says he was with you all morning," I said.

He looked up from some sort of order form he was filling out. "Yah, except for when he delivered the women out to the stands, yes, ma'am, that is correct." Horst's Middle European accent was slight, but noticeable. Unlike Biggs, he was in full deferential mode. I couldn't help but notice that he, too, wore a large hunting knife.

"You see anything unusual today? Anybody skulking around the property?"

He shook his head. "The lodge property is over ten thousand acres, of course. That's nearly fourteen square miles. I wish I could be more helpful, but frankly, it would take an army to stop someone from slipping off or on the property. We catch eight or ten poachers a year. We catch kids trespassing. Yah, there's no telling how many we don't see, don't catch, don't hear, don't even know about." He smiled, but there was no warmth in it. Horst didn't do well at warm and fuzzy.

"Do you mind my asking what line of work you were in before you came to this country?"

"I was in the East German military for fifteen years," he said.

"I had a feeling. Some kind of elite unit, I'm guessing."

"Something like that, yah. After I left the military, I ran a hunting preserve for Communist Party bigwigs in Pomerania, near the Polish border. Once the wall came down, the lodge went broke. So I emigrated to the U.S. in 1991, worked at a hunting property in Texas. Then here."

"You wouldn't mind letting me look at your knife, would you?"

"No, ma'am." He took his knife out of its leather sheath, handed it to me.

"Tell me about it."

"It's Finnish. They call it a *pukko*. As you see, the blade is about fifteen centimeters."

"Five inches, give or take." The simple knife had a round wooden handle, and a tapered blade. Like Biggs's knife, it was very sharp. It was immaculately clean, with no evidence of blood on the blade. I handed it back.

"You have any thoughts on these murders, who might have done them?"

"No, ma'am. I tell you this, I sleep with a gun under my pillow, though." Again, the cold smile.

"Any theories, any thoughts?"

"No, ma'am."

"Nothing whatsoever?"

"No, ma'am."

I squinted at him for a moment. "You don't like speculating much, do you?"

"Yah, this is how I was raised. Don't ask questions, do what you're told." He shrugged. "Horst, the good communist stooge."

I couldn't tell if he was kidding me or not. "According to the case file notes taken by Agent Allgood last year for the Jennifer Treadaway case, a maid named Melima Jakes said that she had washed Jennifer Treadaway's feet, that she cleaned the room of blood, and all that."

"Yah."

"Do you know anything about that?"

"No, ma'am."

"Does she still work here?"

"No, ma'am."

"Can you pull her employment record for me?"

He hesitated briefly, a flicker of resistance in his eye.

"Yes, ma'am," he said finally. Then he swiveled around, tapped some keys on the computer in front of him. A page cycled through the printer. He pulled it out of the bin, handed me a printout listing Melima Jakes's name, address, Social Security number, and earnings for the year. She had made 9,450 dollars as a full-time employee last year.

"There's no phone number on here," I said.

"Most people in Williams County don't have a phone, yah."

"How come she doesn't work here anymore?" I said.

"Terminated."

"You fired her? Why?"

"Melima was slow in the head," he said. "It became a nuisance to Uma. So we got rid of her."

CHAPTER 23

DROVE OUT to the address listed on the piece of paper, and after a good deal of driving around—the numbers on rural routes in Williams County didn't appear to go in any particular order, numerical or otherwise—I found a mailbox with the word JAKES hand-painted on the side in white, dripping letters. I drove up a rutted track, parked when the track ran out, then continued on foot up a sort of trail, which led to a weedy clearing with a rusting, tilted mobile home in the middle. A couple of faded dresses and a towel hung listlessly on a clothes line next to a small garden surrounded by chicken wire.

I knocked on the door. Nobody answered, despite my knocking loudly. But after a minute I heard something behind me and turned to find a small, solidly built black woman standing in the middle of the weedy yard, staring at me with a dull expression on her face. In one hand she carried an ancient shotgun. Hanging from her other hand was a dead rabbit, which she held by the ears.

"Ms. Jakes?" I said. "Melima Jakes?"

"You bring me some cheese?" she said pleasantly. "I been needing that cheese."

"I'm sorry, no."

"Oh. Who is you?" she said. "I thought you was that lady with the cheese."

"My name is Sunny Childs. I'm an investigator. I'm looking into the death of Jennifer Treadaway."

"Who?"

"The lady that was killed last year. At the Hellespont Lodge."

She looked at me blankly. Finally something dawned in her eyes. "Oh. That was some kind of mess."

"It was. Do you think we could go inside and talk?"

"Inside what?"

"Your house."

She blinked. "Oh. Yes, ma'am." She walked slowly across the yard, and with a serious expression on her face, walked in the door. I followed her. There was no furniture in the mobile home, other than a pallet on the floor. There was no heat, and cool air blew through a cracked window.

"Melima, can you tell me about the dead woman?"

"Yes, ma'am." She set the dead rabbit on her kitchen counter. It had once been made of Formica, but the plastic had been stripped off, leaving a slab of stained, warped pressboard. She took a knife out of a drawer and proceeded to gut the rabbit.

"Melima?"

"Yes, ma'am?"

"The dead woman? According to the police, you cleaned her up."

"Oh, yes, ma'am. That's what that police said."

"Did you wash her body?"

"Yes, ma'am. She had blood on it."

"Did you take her shoes off and wash her feet?"

"Oh, yes, ma'am, I done it just like that police said to me. He said, you done took her shoes off and washed her feet, ain't that right? And I done said, yessir, I done it just like you told me."

"That's not exactly what I'm asking, though. I'm asking if you took her shoes off?"

"Yes, ma'am."

"Why, Melima?"

THUNK. Melima cut the rabbit's head off. She stuck the guts and the head in a coffee can, threw the coffee can out the window. " 'Cause the po-lice, he done said it."

"The policeman said you were supposed to take her shoes off?"

She looked confused. "I can't remember."

"See, what I'm getting at, according to the police, when they got there, the dead lady's body had already been cleaned. So if it had already been cleaned, they couldn't have told you to do it. Right?"

Melima looked thoughtful. "Yes, ma'am. That's right."

I was starting to get a little frustrated.

Melima hung the dead rabbit on a rusty hook screwed into the wall. "I always hangs 'em up a day or two. Tenders 'em up."

"Melima, I'm missing a step here. Forget about the police for a minute, just tell me exactly what happened. When you found the dead lady and how you cleaned her up."

"Yes, ma'am. I come in at my usual time. Six o'clock. And they was all the ladies. And it was that one lady, the dead lady, lying on the floor. And one of the big ladies up there at the lodge, she says to me,

Melima, it ain't no good of a dead lady being on the floor, so you needs to clean this up."

"Okay, okay, hold on," I said. "Which lady told you to do this?"

"One of the big ladies."

"What was her name?"

"I don't recollect. It could have been that lady with the red hair."

"There are two ladies with red hair at the lodge. One is named Martha Herrington and the other is named Miranda Wiseberg."

"Yes, ma'am, that's right."

"So which one was it?"

"Yes, ma'am, it was that one."

"Mrs. Herrington?"

"That's right."

"Or Mrs. Wiseberg?"

"That's right, it was her. With the red hair."

I sighed loudly. "One is a big tall woman, the other is built more like me," I said.

"It was that skinny one." She looked at me for a moment. "You and her favor, ain't that funny?"

"Mrs. Wiseberg is my mother."

"Well, ain't that nice. I wish I had me a rich lady for a mama." She looked around the mobile home. "My mama dead. I get all sad sometimes. I get to thinking about that dead lady and my mama and I just get to crying."

"So what happened after Mrs. Wiseberg told you to clean up?"

"I done cleaned the floor. That lady done bled like a stuck pig. Hoooo." She looked out the window, stared off into the woods. "I had me a pig once. It done run off in the woods. I ain't seen it since. Keep thinking I'ma look out there one day, that old hog just gonna come walking right out the woods."

"Okay. So you cleaned the floor. What about the dead lady? What did you do with her?"

Melima bit her lip, frowned. "For true, I ain't remember exactly. Don't seem like I wanted to touch no dead lady."

"So did you clean her body or not?"

"Yes, ma'am."

"You did. Or you didn't?"

"No, ma'am. I ain't like to touch no dead people. My mama done died, I let her sleep for a week before I could do nothing about it. Finally I figured I had do the Christian thing, done drug her out and put her in a hole."

She began to cry. Then, like a very young child, she seemed to forget what she'd been crying about.

"So you didn't touch the dead lady."

"No, ma'am."

"You didn't take her shoes off?"

"Can't think why I'd do a thing like that."

"You didn't wash her feet? With bleach?"

Melima blinked. "Bleach? On a lady *feet*? That ain't make no sense!"

"The police report says that you said you washed Jennifer Treadaway's feet with bleach."

"Who?"

"The dead lady."

"Yes, ma'am."

"But you didn't. You didn't wash her feet."

"No, ma'am."

"And when you found her, was she barefoot, or did she have shoes on?"

"Oh, yes, ma'am. She had bare feet. They was all red and sore and lumpy looking. Sad thing, pretty lady like that, had them ugly red feet." Melima laughed, delighted. "That dead lady should of kept them ugly feet hid up inside them shoes!"

I stood there for a minute. "Do you live here by yourself, Melima?" I said finally.

"Yes, ma'am."

"Anybody ever come out here to take care of you?"

"No, ma'am."

"Where do you get food from?"

"Well, I grows some things, shoots me some possum or some rabbit now and again. Plus which that lady from the state, she bring out that cheese."

"Somebody ought to be taking care of you."

She smiled pleasantly, shrugged. "I makes out pretty good, seem like to me."

I smiled back, gave her a hug. "You take care of yourself, Melima."

"Yes, ma'am."

As I walked across the weedy ground back toward the trail leading to my car, I heard the door open behind me. "You sure you ain't bring me no cheese?"

I drove into Hightower to the one wreck of a store that sold everything from feed and shovels to white bread and staple foods. I bought three pounds of flour, three pounds of corn meal, some butter, some canned vegetables, a pound of sliced cheese, and a few other items. When I got back to Melima's trailer, she was gone. The door was open, though, so I left the food on the kitchen counter. Then I walked back to my car and drove away, not quite sure what I had learned.

CHAPTER 24

WHEN I GOT back to the lodge, I found a white Crown Victoria double-parked in front of the entrance. Biggs was standing near the car.

"The GBI's here?" I said.

"It's cop city around here," he said laconically.

"Where are they?"

He pointed at the woods in the direction where Martha Herrington's body had been found. I borrowed an ATV from behind the lodge and headed off into the woods.

When I reached the stand, I parked and walked toward the crime scene, expecting to find Agent Wayne Allgood. Instead I saw a van was parked on the dirt road, three men wearing blue windbreakers standing around it. When they saw me coming, they climbed back inside the van. And as I turned toward the taped-off area, instead of seeing Agent Allgood, I saw a tall man in an immaculate dark suit working inside the crime scene tape, his trouser cuffs neatly tucked into a pair of rubber boots. His white hair was cut like a Marine drill sergeant's: short on top, shaved on the sides.

A couple of sheriff's deputies were standing around the crime scene tape at parade rest, looking nervous and uncomfortable. As I approached, one of the deputies said, "You can't go in there, Miz Childs."

"Do you know his name?" I said, pointing at the man I presumed to be the GBI agent assigned to the case.

"Mills. But I don't think you want to—"

"Agent Mills!" I called out. The white-haired man turned and looked at me. Because of his white hair, I had assumed he must be in his sixties. But now that I saw his face, I guessed he was less than a decade older than me, mid-forties, but with prematurely white hair. He had the sort of piercing blue-white eyes that seem to cut through you like laser beams. He stared impassively at me for a long moment, then went back to whatever he was doing. He had some sort of electronic box in his hand, which he was waving slowly over the ground.

Just to let him know I wasn't going to be ignored, thank you very much, I lifted the crime scene tape, took one step inside the scene. "Agent Mills!" I said sharply.

"*Oh* hell," said one of the deputies quietly.

"You done it now," another whispered.

The man with the white hair looked up again, met my eyes, and stared at me for a while, his face so expressionless as to seem almost dead. Finally he stood up and walked toward me, a slow gunslinger's swagger. When he finally spoke, his voice was very soft, almost inaudible. "Get off my crime scene," he said.

I put out my hand. "I'm Sunny Childs," I said. "I'm a private investigator retained by the lodge."

His eyes never left mine. "I don't care who or what you are. Get off my crime scene."

Now I was pissed. "Where's Agent Allgood?"

"That's not your concern." He turned to one of the deputies. "Sheriff, if this woman doesn't step behind that tape, place her under arrest for obstruction of justice."

I gave it a moment, then I stepped grudgingly behind the tape. "Agent Mills," I said, "I've conducted an extensive investigation regarding the Treadaway case, and have interviewed most of the lodge guests and employees who were here today. I was thinking I could help get you up to speed on—"

"When I need your help," Agent Mills said, "I will tell you. Sheriff? Escort this woman back to the lodge."

He wheeled around and walked back to whatever he had been doing before my arrival.

"Nice meeting you, too," I shouted.

The deputy nearest me shook his head slowly. "I done told you, Miz Childs. I done told you."

As I retreated to my ATV, face burning, I pulled out my cell and called Wayne Allgood at the Macon GBI office. "Sunny Childs, here," I said. "So who's this jerk they sent to work on the Herrington case?"

"I can't talk about it, Sunny," he said. He sounded angry.

"What's that mean?"

"It means what it says," he said sharply. "The Herrington case has been allocated to another law enforcement resource."

"What about Treadaway? You still have Treadaway?"

"Treadaway has been reallocated, too."

There was a long pause. "Did I get you in trouble?" I said finally.

"I got myself in trouble. I should never have talked to you. But that's on me."

"Why? Why would they reassign this case?"

He cleared his throat.

"Come on, Wayne. Something has changed here. What's changed?"

"Be careful, Sunny. That's all I'm going to say."

After that I heard a click and then dead air.

I frowned at the phone, then redialed the main number for the Macon GBI office. "Agent Mills, please," I said.

"Who?"

"Agent Mills, please."

"I'm sorry," the receptionist said. "There's no Agent Mills here. Which field office is he assigned to?"

CHAPTER 25

I T WAS ABOUT time for dinner, so I went into the Grill Room. Most of the seats were taken, and my mother wasn't in the room, so I sat down across from Emily Stubbins, the anthropology professor from Emory.

"It just gets worse and worse, doesn't it?" she said morosely.

I nodded. She had been out hunting most of the day, so I hadn't had a chance to speak with her yet.

"Found anything out yet?" she said.

"Not really. I interviewed most of the people who'd seen Martha this morning, but nobody had anything useful to tell me." I bit into my deer burger. It was a little gamy and a little dry for my taste. Maybe it was the pressure, or the horror of seeing the dead woman finally catching up to me, or the stress of the encounter with Agent Mills, or maybe it was just the taste of the deer burger—but I felt slightly nauseated. I set the burger down. "How about you?" I said. "Did you see Martha this morning?"

"Yeah, I did," she said.

"When?"

"Well, I saw her at breakfast. But then later I saw her with Biggs."

"Out at her stand?"

She looked puzzled. "At her stand? No, they were over at the shed." She studied my face for a minute. "You know that shed they keep the tractors and cars in? The big metal building? There's a big feed patch over there. Clover. I've harvested a nice buck over there every year." She lowered her voice. "I have a stand over there that nobody knows about. I carry my own tree stand. It's against lodge regulations to use self-climbing tree stands, but I don't really care about lodge regulations." She laughed softly.

"So what did you see?"

"Well, it was about five-thirty, quarter to six. Like I say, I was using a self-climbing stand. You put it around a pine tree, and the way it's designed, you can sort of shinny up the tree with it until you get to whatever height you want. Then you just sit on it. I like self-climbers because you aren't stuck with a location. Half of the stands on the property, the deer know they're there, so they just creep around them. I don't even like to use an all-terrain vehicle to get to my stand. I just hike out there, nice and slow and quiet. Even if it takes an hour to get to my tree and up into the stand, it's worth it. Nothing irks me more than sitting there in the middle of the woods and here comes some moron on an ATV, thinking they own the woods, scaring off every deer in South Georgia."

"You were saying about Biggs and Martha."

"Right, right, sorry. Anyway, I was halfway up the tree when I heard something. That stupid golf cart thing, that pulls the little tram? I heard it coming down the trail. So I stopped moving because, like I say, self-climbing stands are against lodge regulations and I didn't want anybody seeing me. I'd gotten a little bit of a late start, so the sun wasn't quite up. But the sky was getting light. Enough that I could see that it was Biggs driving the cart and Martha in the back.

"So they pulled up to the garage or shed or whatever you want to call it, and they both got out and went inside. I took the opportunity to get my stand up to where I want it. Twenty feet or so up the tree. About that time, they came back out the door. But now they were arguing. My stand was about a hundred and ten, a hundred and twenty yards away from the shed, so I couldn't hear exactly what they were saying. But they were making a lot of noise. I was kind of pissed, because I figured they'd scare away the deer, waste my morning.

"I carry a pair of pocket binoculars, of course, so I glassed them. She was waving her hands and yelling, and he was yelling back. Finally she smacked him in the face. You know what a spooky-looking guy he is, right? Well, at that point he stopped talking. He just stood there and stared at her with those creepy black eyes of his, didn't say a word. She kept yelling, but he didn't move a muscle.

"Finally it was like she ran out of gas. She just turned around and walked up the path. And the whole time she was walking, he was watching her. Watching and watching and not moving a muscle."

She stopped her narrative, picked up her fork, and sawed off a large piece of deer.

"What then?" I said.

Emily Stubbins chewed, shrugged. "Mmmhimp," she said.

"What?"

More chewing. Emily swallowed. "Nothing. Then nothing. She disappeared down the trail. He went back inside. Then after a few minutes he got back on an ATV that was parked beside the shed, and headed back down the trail."

"Which direction?"

"Same way he'd come."

"Which was the same direction that Martha had gone, right?"

Emily Stubbins ate another piece of venison and some peas, then nodded. "Yes. I guess you could say that. He went back down the trail toward her. But I mean she was long gone by then."

We ate in silence for a while. That is, Emily ate and I sat there pushing my food around my plate and trying not to feel too nauseated.

"Anybody around here with a motive for killing her?"

Emily Stubbins suddenly seemed more cheerful. "Isn't this lodge just the strangest thing in the world?" she said.

I made some sort of noncommittal noise. I didn't see what her comment had to do with my question.

"I don't publish much anymore," the professor said, "but I did my early research on the social dynamics of female groups. I grew up in a family with a bunch of boys, all of them more macho than the next, and so I've never been all that comfortable around groups of women. I suppose I did my research for that very reason: I was trying to understand why it was that I always felt so out of place among women. Don't get me wrong, I have female friends. And I do fine woman-to-woman. But big groups of women drive me batty."

"I think most women feel that way," I said. "We all talk about how nurturing and sharing women are, and then you get five or six of us together and here comes the backbiting and the pettiness and all the nasty little games."

Emily Stubbins laughed loudly. "Ain't it the truth, sister."

"As a trained anthropologist, you must find this bunch particularly interesting." I waved my finger around the room. "The thought must have crossed your mind at least once that a bunch of gold diggers would make for a pretty interesting study."

Another loud laugh. "More than once, believe me." She swabbed some gravy off her plate with a biscuit. "Actually, to be boringly pedagogical for a moment, it's less the anthropology than the psychology of this group that I find interesting."

"How so?"

"Deer, as you know, are rather placid, wimpy little creatures throughout most of the year. But male deer begin producing massive amounts of testosterone in the late summer, at which point they begin to grow large phallic-looking things out of their heads, they begin to strut and compete for status, their necks begin to swell and engorge with blood. Once their antlers are fully developed and hardened, they begin flinging them-selves at each other in ritual battle and having sex with anything that moves."

"And that has to do with female psychology in what way?"

She laughed. "Oh, come on, Sunny! Don't play the naif. Hunting season corresponds with rutting season." She waved her hand at all of the women. "Huntresses! Stalking the woods for a big buck, its muscles engorged with blood, these huge phallic things sticking out of its head, its veins coursing with testosterone! We take our tools into the woods and we attempt to seduce and subdue the most powerful, most male thing in the woods." She raised her eyebrows. "What could be a more perfect metaphor for this bunch of gold diggers."

"I suppose you're right," I said.

"I mean seriously, it's terribly unfashionable, but these women are, in a way, the *ne plus ultra* of womanhood. Don't let Gloria Steinhem fool you: being a woman is all about bagging the biggest, fattest, toughest, horniest buck in the woods. Anybody who tells you different is so deeply full of crap it's not even funny."

"What about child-rearing and nurturing and all that?"

She dismissed this with a flick of her fork. "Men want sex, women want mates. Anything beyond that is an evolutionary aftereffect." She stood, leaving her empty plate and a large pile of crumbs.

"I asked you if you knew of anybody with a motive, and you dodged my question," I said.

"I thought I *was* answering your question. I know, I know, we academics never answer a question except with a question. What I was getting at is this—the foremost rule of female behavior: never stand between a woman and her intended mate."

I laughed. "So you think that one of the women here killed them because of some kind of jealousy thing?"

"It is, as we say, a theory."

"Well, I guess that's more than I had before."

Emily Stubbins got up and then said, "Oh, I forgot. One more thing about Biggs. After he drove off in the ATV, he came back. Couldn't have been more than five minutes later. Then he threw something into the woods, hopped back on the golf cart, and drove away."

CHAPTER 26

I DECIDED TO go ahead and confront Biggs, see what he said when I told him that he had lied about delivering Martha Herrington directly to her tree. I went to the gun room, but he wasn't there, so I checked the area where he cleaned deer—but the only person there was Alf, a grizzled old black man with an unlit cigar stub perpetually sticking out of his mouth.

"You seen Biggs?" I said.

"Not lately, ma'am. That white-headed FBI agent come by a while back, wanted to ax him some questions."

"GBI, you mean."

He shrugged. "FBI, GBI, all the same to me."

I went back into the lodge, going room to room until I heard Biggs's voice. Then I spotted them through the window, standing behind a screen of bushes next to the gravel drive. The white-haired GBI man was standing over Biggs, giving him a hard look. I slipped around the corner and out the door where I could hear them, but they couldn't see me.

"I ain't telling you jack," Biggs was saying.

Agent Mills glared down at him. "I'll have you hauled off to jail."

"For what?"

"Place him under arrest."

One of the guys in the blue windbreakers cranked Biggs's arms behind his back, put a pair of cuffs on him.

"Sir," the agent in the blue windbreaker said, "you are under arrest for being a felon in possession of a firearm."

"What you might want to do, before I file the lawsuit," Biggs said, smiling, "is check down at the state. You'll find that I got what they call a limited pardon. I appealed to the governor for clemency due to my line of work, said I'd lose my livelihood if I couldn't use firearms. One of these nice ladies here at the lodge, her husband was the governor's personal lawyer, put in a good word for me. Worked like a charm. It's not a general pardon, it just makes it legal for me to carry a pistol, shotgun, rifle, whatever I choose to."

The white haired agent's blue eyes didn't waver. One of his henchmen cranked Biggs's arms up another notch, making Biggs grimace.

"Come to think of it," Biggs hissed, "I got a copy of the pardon back in my room."

Agent Mills nodded at one of the other agents. "Go."

"Top drawer of my desk," Biggs called. "Underneath the naked pictures of your mama!"

They waited in silence. Four or five minutes later, the agent came back with a piece of paper, which he handed to Agent Mills. Mills read it silently, then said, "Take the cuffs off."

"I want a damn apology," Biggs said. "False arrest, man. I'll have your badge."

Mills ignored him. "How long were you alone with the victim?" Mills said.

"You got a hearing problem, you moron?" Biggs said. "I ain't telling you nothing."

The second agent slid a thin black glove onto his hand, gave Biggs a karate chop across the side of the head. Biggs fell down on the floor.

"Go ahead," he said, wiping blood off the side of his face. "Do it again. Then watch how fast I call my lawyer."

"Don't do that again, Agent Rice," Mills said. "Now take his cuffs off."

The agent flushed. "Yessir." The guy in the wind-breaker leaned over, took the cuffs off.

Agent Mills kept looking down at Biggs. Finally he said, "We're done with you, Biggs. For now."

Then he whirled and walked back to his car. The three agents in windbreakers followed him across the gravel, climbed into their white van, then they all drove away.

I walked over to Biggs, handed him a Kleenex.

"I saw it happen," I said. "If you need a witness or something."

Biggs gave me a small, bitter smile. "You the good cop, huh?"

"What's that supposed to mean?"

"Me being the one person around here with a criminal record? My mama didn't raise no fool. If it ain't Mr. FBI there that tries to take me down for them murders, it's gonna be you."

I didn't say anything.

"I know how you people do it. Flit your eyes around,

show me a little cleavage, I'm s'pose to turn into jelly?
Not likely." He stood up and began walking back toward the lodge.

"You're welcome!" I called to him.

He didn't answer.

I ran after him, cut him off before he got to the door.
"Okay, fair enough," I said. "How about I play bad
cop for a minute."

His black eyes fixed themselves on my face. "Get
out of my way."

"I know you were with Martha Herrington this
morning down at the shed. Don't bother lying to me."

"I'm telling you the same thing I told that white-
haired shit-ass. Which is, nothing."

"You want me to go tell Agent Mills what I know?
That you took Martha Herrington to the shed? That the
two of you had a fight? That she slapped you in the
face? That she walked off and then you drove after
her?"

His black eyes stared at me for a long time. "Get
out of my way," he said finally.

"I'm a nice person," I said. "You give me a reason-
able explanation for what you were doing, I'm happy
to accept it, let the whole thing pass." I spread my
hands. "But Agent Mills? I don't know if he's going
to be quite as quick to let it go."

He shoved past me, digging an elbow into my ribs
as he disappeared through the door.

CHAPTER 27

THE NEXT MORNING I was up at four. I dressed my-self in head-to-toe camouflage, and headed out into the dark, silent woods. A week earlier I had hidden in some bushes and watched Biggs drive away from the big shed in a Mercedes. Since I had nothing much else to do, I figured I might as well find the same bushes, park myself there with a pair of binoculars, and see what happened. The shed was about a mile away. It was still dark when I got there.

I sat quietly on a rock and tried to be as still as possible. For a while the woods were almost com-pletely silent, nothing moving but the soft wind in the tops of the trees. Gradually birds began making noises, piping and cooing all around me. Then I heard a soft crunching noise, a foot moving in the leaves to my left. The noise stopped. What if Biggs (or somebody else?) had heard me leave and had followed me down here?

Another crunch. Then silence. I strained my senses, trying to see or hear or smell something. I smelled loam and pine and something vaguely animal. There was a crunch to my right. I swiveled my head, but it was so dark I couldn't see anything but vague grada-tions of black.

Something moved in front of me. My heart rate began rising. I thought for a moment that I heard breathing, but then I strained and strained and there was nothing but the soft shushing of the wind.

Another footfall to my left. Growing closer, coming toward me. Another. Then silence again.

The silence seemed to stretch on forever. The air was chilly, dry. I shivered slightly.

And then suddenly but somehow imperceptibly, the light changed. There, where just moments before the sky had been black, punctuated by the long thin black trunks of trees, lay an infinitely modest but recognizably pale haze.

And in that pallid light, there they were. All around me. At least seven or eight deer—some does and some fawns. I felt a rush of goodwill and gratitude—though what I felt grateful for, I couldn't precisely say. I watched through the holes in my camouflage face mask as they delicately nibbled at shoots of greenbriar and blackberry vine.

Then, in the distance, I saw a flash of something white, appearing and disappearing behind a row of brambles. At first I thought I was imagining it. But then, out of the corner of my eye, I saw the flash again, this time a few feet closer. I stared right where I'd seen the motion. There was a pale patch of something, but I couldn't make out what it was. I stared and stared. For a moment I imagined it was the pale face of Raiford Biggs. But then I saw a slight motion and what had seemed to be a tangle of branches became the massive twisted antlers of the deer they called Moby Dick, the big white buck.

The white deer, I realized, was staring straight at me.

We stared at each other for a long time, then his tail went up and he bounded noisily off into the brush. Around me all the other deer's heads went up, then their white tails flashed and the woods were noisy with hoofbeats, and then they were all gone and I was alone in the silence.

I sat and sat and sat, my arms growing stiff, my back sore, the urge to get up and run off into the woods building and building like steam pressure. Anything for motion, for freedom, for an end to the waiting. I resisted that pressure, though.

And then at ten o'clock, the waiting paid off. Just as it had happened the previous week, a plane flew over, low and slow. It was a single-engine prop plane, with landing gear permanently extended. It was low enough that I was able to see the tail number. I repeated the number in my mind a couple of times, committing it to memory. After a short while, the plane came back over my head, gaining altitude, heading up into the sky again.

Ten minutes later, a white panel truck pulled slowly down the rutted dirt road, one of the automatic bay doors rose, and the truck disappeared into the shed. Because of the angle of the sun, the windshield was a sheet of glare and I couldn't see the driver. But I figured it was probably Biggs, just like last time. The bay door scrolled slowly down behind the truck.

A few minutes later, the bay door slowly opened and a long black Mercedes emerged—again, the same one that Biggs had driven last time. The Mercedes charged up the dirt road, spitting rocks, the bay door slowly, slowly closing behind it.

Suddenly something occurred to me. I was sixty yards away, and the huge bay door was still half open. I began sprinting toward it, reaching it just in time to hurl myself on the ground and spin underneath it, just like some action movie heroine.

What they don't show in the movies is how much it hurts to do things like that. I stood up slowly, my head aching from where I'd banged it on the floor, my left sleeve torn to reveal a four-inch-long concrete burn, oozing tiny beads of blood.

The big bay door made a last grinding noise, then stopped.

I had made the sprint with no clear goal in mind. But once I got there, a plan formed in my mind. Over on the far side of the room was my mother's Jaguar—the one I'd driven off the road when I was coming up. Apparently they had stored it here, waiting for me or Mom to make arrangements to have it fixed. The fenders were still folded like an accordion, but I knew from previous experience that it still ran. And I had a key for it in my fanny pack.

I ran over to the last bay door and pressed a large green button on the wall. As the bay door began slowly rising, I hopped into Mom's Jag, started the engine.

Ten minutes later I pulled up to a two-lane road. Which way? Left, I figured, then drove in the direction of the main entrance to the lodge, to the county seat, and after that to the interstate. Right led who knows where. I drove the Jag as hard as it would go. I'm told those English engineers aren't much for reliability—but they sure know something about handling and power. By the time the two-lane road joined up with I-75, I had spotted the long black Mercedes. It took the on-ramp heading north toward Atlanta.

I figured, what the hell. I took the on-ramp toward Atlanta, too.

The next couple of hours were uneventful. The Mercedes drove at a steady three miles an hour over the speed limit—slower than prevailing traffic on the laxly policed Georgia highways, but not slow enough to attract attention.

Everything was fine up through Macon and the suburbs of Atlanta. But by the time we reached the city of Atlanta proper, I was starting to get nervous. The orange LOW FUEL light had come on and the gauge needle was below empty. If I stopped for gas, though, I knew I would lose Biggs. And whatever I had hoped to accomplish by following him would be lost: I'd have thrown away the whole morning for nothing.

So it gave me a sense of some relief when the black Mercedes put on its blinker and turned off at the exit for The Ted—the Braves baseball stadium named after Ted Turner. Ted Turner Field is situated in the middle of an area that's not exactly what you would call prime real estate. It's down on the south side of down, a very poor neighborhood that had once been a blue-collar industrial area and was now mostly just blighted. There had been some rehabbing and sprucing up as a result of the stadium—but that lasted for only a couple of blocks. The black Mercedes barreled down the street past the stadium and off into southeast Atlanta.

It was not exactly Mercedes and Jaguar country. I felt pretty conspicuous as I headed down the road. It was a delicate balance, trying to keep Biggs in sight while not staying too close.

My LOW FUEL light was blinking steadily as we headed through a neighborhood full of aging cars, boarded-up houses, and crumbling commercial buildings surrounded by rusting, barbed wire–topped fences. I didn't really relish hiking through this part of town with a gas can in my hands, and I didn't have my cell phone to call for assistance.

Nervous or not, there was no choice but to press on.

I was not so nervous, though, that I wasn't moved to wonder what sort of business a hunting guide from south Georgia was conducting in the middle of south Atlanta.

Suddenly the Mercedes's blinker went on and it pulled a hard right into a gap in a long stretch of rusting fence. At least Biggs used his blinker. He was probably the only guy in the state who did. I don't know what it is about Georgians, but we seem to think that the blinker stalk is useful only as a rack to hang air freshener off of.

I drove past the fence, past a concrete block bunker of a building, turned right, and attempted to circle the block. I say "attempted" because the Jag made a number of funny noises and then lost all power. Out of gas.

I jumped out of the car and ran over to the corner of the old warehouse, peeped through a gap in the fence. The Mercedes was just pulling up to the loading dock, where a man in a loud green silk suit was standing. His hair was dyed blond and spiked up in the sort of awful-looking hairdo you'd expect to see on the ugliest singer in some third-rate boy band.

The door of the Mercedes opened and out climbed— I had been so sure that it would be Biggs getting out of the car, that I didn't quite recognize who it was. It

was a woman, blond, wearing a fur coat, fashionable
little sunglasses, very high heels, and a clingy dress
made of something that looked like gold Saran wrap.
Her face was very attractive, but with far too much
makeup—bright red lipstick, dark lip liner, two shades
of eyeshadow, enough eyeliner for a Wagnerian so-
prano, and a half bucket of blush. It was what I think
of as the Russian New Money look. But of course, she
wasn't Russian. She was East German.

It was Uma Krens.

Martha Herrington had told me that she was a mute,
incapable of speech—but judging by the amiable conversation she struck up with the boy band singer, she
had miraculously learned to speak on the road up from
Atlanta.

After they had chatted briefly, the boy band singer
looked carefully around the large empty parking lot,
his eyes narrowed suspiciously. I ducked back behind
the wall. When I peeked out again, Boy Band was pulling out a cell phone, with which he made a brief call.
Within a minute, a red BMW had pulled inside the
fence. It made a hard turn, then backed up quickly but
smoothly to the Mercedes. Uma hit a button on her
keychain, popping the trunk. A very large, muscular
man in a track suit jumped out of the BMW, took a
large Styrofoam cooler out of the rear of the Mercedes,
and transferred it into the trunk of the BMW. He leaned
into the BMW as though inspecting the cooler, then
pulled something out, a squat plastic jar about the size
of a small jar of peanut butter. He tossed it to Boy
Band, who unscrewed the lid, sniffed the jar, then
nodded.

Boy Band walked back into the building, came out

with a cheap fiberglass-shelled briefcase, handed it to Uma. The big man in the track suit slammed both trunks shut, hopped back into the BMW, revved the engine loudly, and drove off, tires squealing and smoking. Uma followed suit—if at a somewhat more sedate pace.

Boy Band watched them go, looked slowly around the parking lot, then went back inside. It was what-to-do time. On the one hand, I could wander around for a while and hope I blundered into a gas station or a taxi before some sort of unpleasant little urban adventure happened to me. Or I could investigate. Investigation was inside the fence. Wandering and blundering were in a neighborhood I didn't know, where I suspected that white women in survivalist costumes were not especially welcome.

I opted to sneak through the fence and try to figure out what Uma had been doing there. There was a hole cut in the fence that I was barely able to fit through; but I made it without tearing more than a couple more holes in my camo shirt. In retrospect, it was a dumb, overconfident, rookie move. But you know what they say about 20–20 hindsight . . .

I walked stealthily across the cracked and weed-split blacktop, climbed the stairs onto the loading dock, and tried the handle of the door.

What was I thinking? I really can't imagine. But the door handle turned, and in I went. I found myself at the end of a long bare hallway, a door on one side opening into a small warehouse space full of metal shelves, most of them empty. I could see Boy Band doing something on the far end of the warehouse, so I figured I had at least a minute or two to poke around.

Slowly, my heart beating hard, I crept down the hallway. Every footstep seemed loud as a gun shot.

At the end of the hallway was a small, drab office.
I turned the handle to the door, slipped inside. There
on the table was the squat plastic jar, the same one I'd
seen the guy in the BMW throw to Boy Band. Looking
closer, I saw that it was, in fact, a peanut butter jar,
with a big picture of a peanut on the front. The label,
oddly enough, was written in Dutch.

I considered the matter: so Uma and Horst and Biggs
were importing really, really, really special and tasty
Dutch peanut butter using light planes which landed at
an air strip in middle Georgia because the world's largest airport—to wit, Atlanta's Hartsfield Airport—was
just not a convenient place through which to import
foreign goods. Hm. Not likely.

I unscrewed the peanut butter jar, turned it upside
down on the desk. A long, gleaming glob of peanut
butter slowly oozed out of the jar and onto the table.
And there, in the middle of the blob, was what it was
all about: a small plastic bag. I pulled the bag open
and about five-hundred tiny blue pills—each with the
letter X molded in the middle of it—scattered in a
shower onto the desk.

Amsterdam, I'm told, is the world's leading produc-
tion center for the illegal drug ecstasy. Street name:
X—the hottest drug in America.

I started to whisper something clever and self-
congratulatory, but I don't remember what it was. All
I remember is the feeling of something shattering in
my head, and the darkness taking me.

• • •

When I recovered consciousness, I was lying on the floor, duct-taped by my hands and feet to the base of one of the metal shelves. It took me a little while to get oriented. My head hurt unmercifully, and I felt sick to my stomach, and there was blood in my mouth. I began screaming. I screamed, "Help!" and I screamed, "Please!" and I just plain old screamed and screamed, no words at all. That went on for a while, but finally I realized there was nobody to hear me.

I lay there for a while finally, exhausted. Then I screamed some more. And then I thought about Barrington Cherry, and how underwhelmed he'd seemed when I'd asked him to marry me. It was almost like he'd been expecting it, some kind of drama, some kind of overblown gesture on my part.

I have dated a long string of jerks and losers and not-quite-right guys, and I'd thought that Barrington was finally *it*, the guy who actually made sense. I loved him. I really did. And yet somehow I'd lost him, and I couldn't even figure out why. I lay there on the floor, my arms duct-taped behind me, weeping, feeling sorry for myself. I could have just flown in from Barbados yesterday, taken a day to straighten up my loft, gone to the bookstore, fixed Barrington a nice meal, had a drink, relax. I could have done anything I pleased, anything that Barrington pleased, anything at all. Yet here I was.

Why? Why was I here instead of back home with Barrington? I couldn't even vaguely come up with an answer. In my state, lying there on that floor, I stopped feeling afraid. The fear was replaced by a feeling of shame and incomprehension.

And then the door opened and the big weightlifter,

the one who had been driving the BMW, came in.

"How long have I been here?" I said.

He ignored me. There was a sense of immense physical competence about him, like some former Olympic wrestler or judo man. His face was impassive, plain as a brick, and his brown hair was jelled into fey little ringlets. He wore a heavy gold watch on one large wrist.

Crossing the room, he picked up a folding chair, set it in the middle of the warehouse. Then he came over, cut me free from the shelf with a switchblade knife, and picked me up. I didn't even bother trying to struggle until he set me down in the chair. When I saw that he was about to tape me to the chair, I began squirming. He put one of his massive hands around my neck and shook me, his face still as expressionless as a man watering his garden. I couldn't believe how strong he was. He literally lifted me and the chair off the ground and shook me like a dog.

"Okay, okay, okay, I get the picture," I said.

He set me down, finished securing me to the chair, wrapping my torso with layer after layer of plastic dry-cleaning bags. Then he rolled a red metal tool case over next to me, the kind on casters that auto mechanics use. When he had the tool case where he wanted it, he took off his fancy watch and set it carefully on top of the tool case, then stood at parade rest, staring at the wall, as though waiting to be reviewed by a general from headquarters.

After a while Boy Band breezed in.

"At ease, Werner," he said crisply.

I hadn't noticed it before, but there was something military in Boy Band's bearing, something at odds with his flamboyant, not-quite-hip costume. Like Horst, he had a German accent.

"Sunny Childs," he said, with only a whisper of a German accent. Boy Band was looking at a spot about six inches above me head. "Age thirty-four. Five feet even, one hundred and one pounds, licensed private investigator, graduate of Bryn Mawr College with a degree in economics. Spent two years on Wall Street before returning to your home town of Atlanta. Father, believed KIA in Vietnam; mother, remarried four times—a rather impressive record if I may say so— and a well-to-do socialite."

"Okay," I said. "So you can use a computer."

"Hit her."

Werner did as he was told, slapping me across the face with a hand that was as hard as a board. The chair and I fell over. My left ear rang from the blow.

"I know all I need to know about you," Boy Band said, looking off into the air. "What I will now find out is what *you* know about *me*."

"I know you're an asshole."

"Ah, you're a wit, too." Boy Band smiled. "Werner, lift her up again."

Werner lifted the chair, setting me upright. Boy Band had two faces and two smiles, and they were spinning slowly past me without ever quite moving. I felt like I might throw up any second.

"Who have you told?"

"Nobody," I said.

"Werner."

"Wait! Wait!" I cringed, steeling for the blow.

Boy Band lifted his hand slightly and Werner backed up half a pace.

"This is the point in the movie where the bad guy always says something like, 'Oh, my dear, this is so distasteful,' " The two Boy Bands smiled. "Except that, actually, I don't think it's distasteful at all. I kind of enjoy it. And Werner? Well, I don't know if he enjoys it or not. But that's okay, because Werner's not an ego-driven person. He just does what I say, and I suppose that makes him feel wanted and needed and whole. Right, Werner?"

Werner didn't seem to feel obliged to reply to this.

"Look," I said. "I suspected Biggs of something, but I didn't know what. I followed Uma here, saw you guys do the exchange, snuck in here. That's it. I didn't tell anybody."

"Chair please, Werner."

Werner moved quickly across the room, came back with a second folding chair, which he set in front of me. Boy Band sat down, then scooched the chair forward until our knees touched.

"You're really a remarkably stupid woman," he said.

"I couldn't agree more," I said.

"If you came in here without telling anyone, you're a fool. On the other hand, if you did tell someone, and you think that you can stall for time, blah blah blah, while you wait for them to show up, then you're also an idiot. Now: who did you tell?"

"Nobody."

Boy Band nodded at Werner. Werner opened the top drawer of the tool chest, began pulling things out and lining them up on the lid of the chest: a pair of pliers, a rusting screwdriver that had been ground to a rough point, a piece of thin rubber hose, a couple of syringes still in the factory plastic wrap, two ampules of clear liquid, a socket wrench, and an oil-stained rag. He wrapped the rag around the socket wrench, and set it back on top of the red tool case, then slipped one of the syringes out of its plastic wrap and held it toward Boy Band.

Boy Band picked up an ampule, snapped the glass top off, then inserted the syringe and sucked up most of the liquid through the needle.

"Here it is," Boy Band said. "Back when I was a young trainee in East Germany, they taught us two routes to the truth. In interrogation class, I'm talking about." He took the syringe from Werner, held it up in front of me. "The subtle route." Then he picked up the pair of pliers. "And the not-so-subtle route."

"I swear I didn't tell anybody."

"Give me something useful, some little grain of truth, and I'll go the subtle route. But if you continue being intransigent, I'll start by extracting your teeth and then move on to removing your fingers." He slammed the pliers down on the red painted metal.

"You really don't want to do this," I said. "My boyfriend's in the FBI."

Boy Band grinned at Werner. "The old my-boyfriend's-in-the-FBI ploy! Oh, that's a terrific one. Marvelous! Bravo!"

"Check your computer again," I said. "I'm serious."

"Just for that, I think I'll go with the not-so-subtle approach."

Just as he was reaching for the pliers again, Boy Band's cell phone rang. "What!" he said irritably into the phone. Then he sighed and rolled his eyes, flipped the phone shut, and said something in German to Werner. I don't speak German, but I got the impression he was saying something to the effect of, "Something's come up that I have to handle. Watch her until I get back."

He turned and walked briskly out of the warehouse. A moment later I heard a car motor cranking up.

I've been in a few life-or-death situations before, and one thing I've learned is that the adrenaline rush of blinding fear lasts for only so long. And then a sort of calm comes on you. At least, that's how it is with me. I figured I had until Boy Band got back. If I didn't make a move by then, then I was probably dead.

"Werner," I said after a few minutes. "Werner, I can't breathe."

Werner ignored me.

"Werner, this plastic wrap . . ." I took a couple of gasping little breaths. "Werner, it's tightening up. Your boss isn't going to be ecstatic"—gasp, gasp—"if I"—gasp, gasp, gasp— "suffocate in here."

Werner continued to stare at the wall.

I made some more little gasping noises, speeding them up until I was panting like a dog. Then I let my head slump over.

After a moment Werner said, *"Scheisse."* Then he took his knuckle and dug it into my sternum presumably to see if I was faking. It hurt like crazy, but I managed to keep my eyes closed and just mumble something.

I got the feeling he didn't know what to do. Finally he started unwrapping the plastic wrap. I let my body relax, turn to dead weight. Eventually Werner got all the plastic wrap off me. I slipped off the chair and would have fallen to the floor if Werner hadn't caught me. He bent over me, and set me back on the chair.

I teach a self-defense class for women. It is an article of faith of mine that if you're in a physical altercation with a man, you should kick him in the nuts. I don't know this to be true from personal experience, but whenever I raise the question of its effectiveness with male friends, they wince and then laugh and tell me that no woman has any conception of what real pain is because they will never experience what it's like to be kicked in the testicles.

As ye believe, so shall ye do. As Werner straightened up, I opened my eyes and stomped him as hard as I could between his legs. He grabbed himself and folded up, a noise coming out of his mouth that sounded like a train whistle in a tunnel. I stood shakily, grabbed the loaded syringe off the table, slammed it into his arm, pushed the plunger.

Werner slowly straightened up, his eyes furious, and came toward me. Apparently a kick in the groin only takes you so far. I grabbed the socket wrench off the table, hit him in the head, but he kept coming. I turned and ran for the door, but even hobbling from the pain he was faster. As my hand hit the doorknob into the hallway, his huge arms closed around me.

I expected him to squeeze me, throw me down, something—but instead, nothing: he just picked me up and held me off the floor, my legs dangling helplessly in the air.

I turned my face and looked at him. He showed no sign of pain now. There was a pleasant smile on his face.

"Werner?" I said.

He kept smiling. After a minute, he said, "Yes?"

"Werner, don't hurt me."

Another long pause. "Okay."

I don't know what was in that syringe, but it must have been taking effect.

"Werner, put me down."

Werner set me down slowly. He wasn't smiling now, just looking vague and confused.

"Werner, go sit in that chair." I pointed at the chair sitting in the middle of a pile of plastic.

He frowned, then turned and hobbled slowly across the room.

"I'm going now," I said.

And I did. Within seconds I was in the parking lot and running toward the gate leading to the street, a feeling of euphoria coursing through me.

The euphoria lasted about three seconds. Because that's when the red BMW turned in off the street and began barreling toward me, Boy Band at the wheel.

I turned and ran the other way, heading toward the gap in the fence. Behind me the BMW screeched to a halt and the car door opened. I rammed through the little hole in the fence.

I heard footsteps racing toward me, accompanied by some harsh, glottal sounds that were undoubtedly German curse words. Something slammed into the fence. Boy Band's arm came through the hole, but the hole was too small for him. The arm disappeared and then the fence began shaking as he began to scale it. I stumbled backward into the street.

I heard something then, but I was so confused and preoccupied with getting away from Boy Band, that it took my frazzled brain a moment to process the sound.

It was a car horn. Accompanied by a shrieking of brakes.

Which is when I realized that I was in the path of an onrushing vehicle. I turned and saw an old school bus, painted white, heading straight toward me. I froze. It barreled closer and closer, skidding sideways on the pavement as the driver attempted to stop. Something in my mind was shouting *Get out of the way! Get out of the way!* But the part of my brain responsible for moving my feet didn't seem to be listening. The bus grew closer and closer.

Finally, it shuddered to a halt, the grill of the bus stopping not more than two feet from my face. Painted across the front of the bus was a sign that said CHURCH OF THE UNRESERVED WORD. I could hear people inside the bus clapping and singing hymns.

Behind me a hand came over the top of the fence. Then some dyed blond hair. Then another hand, this one clutching a pistol.

I ran around to the door of the bus, banged on it with the flat of my hand. The driver opened the door slowly, a suspicious look on his face. I ran onto the bus. Two long rows of dark faces stared up at me. The singing and clapping had stopped. It seemed like an awfully long time went by. I imagined what they must have thought seeing a little skinny white woman in head-to-toe camouflage standing there in the middle of southeast Atlanta.

I don't know how long I stood there. Probably not long at all. But it seemed to drag on forever and ever.

"Folks," I said finally, "I'm ready for salvation!"

Silence.

"Want to head for that perfect shore!" I shouted.

"Praise God!" an old woman in an elaborate feathered hat said, raising her arms over her head. On the other side of the road I saw Boy Band dropping off the fence. Everyone in the bus was looking at me, so they didn't notice him as he charged toward us.

"You don't mind driving right on, do you?" I said to the driver. "I got a strong feeling coming on me." I dropped to my knees and waved my hands in the air, just like the old lady in the feather hat had done, letting my fingers sway gently like seaweed in an ocean current. I was kind of making a little show, just to get the bus moving. But I was also feeling funny in a way I couldn't quite explain.

"Tell it!" said the old woman in the feathered hat.

"Don't make me wait!" I said. "Oh, I feel it! I feel it!"

"You just go head on, sister!" the driver said. "Let it out!"

Then he pressed the pedal, and I watched as Boy Band receded in the sideview mirror, sprinting down the middle of the road waving his pistol and cursing.

CHAPTER 28

I N RETROSPECT, I feel strange—maybe a little guilty even—about what happened next, like I was abusing the trust of people who believed I meant one thing, when, in fact, I meant something else altogether. But whoever it is that's in charge of things around here does indeed work in mysterious ways, and so in the grand scheme I'm not sure that I have anything to be sorry about.

What I'm saying is that by the time we reached the little storefront church where they were about to have an afternoon service, I was crying and shaking and feeling generally out of control of myself. For those of you who have never been beaten, or had a gun pulled on you, or been threatened with torture and death by psychopaths, this might seem a little extreme. But if you have had any of these things happen, you'll know exactly the feeling, the sense I had that my entire brain had been picked up, shaken, and thrown back down.

What happened next comes back to me only in bits and pieces, but here's what I remember: a crowd of large women led me up to the front of the small room in a storefront church, past a bunch of people sitting on folding chairs. There was a band playing—an organ and a bass and drummer—and people were clapping and shouting. And then a tall, consumptive-looking preacher with a pencil mustache and processed hair and a gold suit took me in his arms and hugged me and said something about strangers and baskets made of rushes floating on wide, muddy rivers, and the peculiar ways in which the Lord threw things out to people in their times of deepest need, and how there was no predicting the course of that wide, muddy river but only of trusting in its current. And then there were some Amens from the people in the room. And then there was a long, long, long song, with a lot of clapping and shouting, and people were touching me and holding me as I cried and clapped my hands in time to the music.

And when it was over, the tall thin preacher asked if I wished to witness, now that I had given up my soul to Jesus.

I didn't precisely remember having given up my soul to Jesus, but nevertheless I felt moved to say something.

"Yes," I said. "I think I need to bear witness."

Then the room got quiet, forty or fifty people just looking at me. And then something happened in me, a feeling like something was being opened up, unfurling inside me like a flower.

"What's it mean to be a witness?" I said. "What's it mean to see a thing, and then tell it? What's it mean?"

And the organist hit a chord, a minor seventh, just brushing the keys and letting it go.

"Tell it!" said the old lady in the feathered hat. Everyone else sat, but she was standing up there in the front row, waving a handkerchief slowly back and forth in the air.

"There's something wrong in my life," I said. "A hole. It's been there for so long I almost don't see it anymore."

"Yes. Yes." Voices from the back of the room.

"There's something wrong, and I couldn't, I couldn't, I couldn't put a name to it or put a finger on it."

"Well!"

"Yes!"

"But now you know!"

"Now you know!"

"Yes!" I said. "Now I know!" I felt a broad smile breaking out on my face, the tears still running hot down my face. "I have been a witness now for too long. I have been standing on the side for too long. I have been watching for too long."

"Yes! Got to jump in!"

"I loved a man, or I thought I loved him, I wanted to commit to him, but I kept pushing him away in subtle and foolish ways. I kept pushing him away because I didn't have my feet on anything solid. He's a strong man. A good man. But a strong man, for sure, and I felt like if I let myself completely open up to him, just let myself relax into him, that he might just swallow me up. Swallow me whole."

"*Mm!*" the organist said. Then he mashed on some keys, not even a chord, just a swirling cacophony of notes.

"All my life I've been a witness. I've been a witness because I haven't had the courage to dive in. I mean, we all can see what's right in front of our faces. The truth, the real thing, the solid thing, people, it's all right there for us. Right in front of us." I held out my hands as though pressing on the base of some great monolith. "But pride and embarrassment and uncertainty and fear—they kept holding me back."

The room was silent again. I wasn't sure if they were with me or not, but I felt something pressing me on.

"What are we so afraid of, people?"

Some heads nodded. The organist gave me another chord and the drummer did a little *ssshhhhhwhomp!* on the snare.

"I saw a woman killed this week. Just yesterday. And now I think I know why. Maybe not exactly why, but I'm beginning to see the outlines. She was a witness, but she couldn't tell what she saw. She was afraid to stand up, to fess up, to move forward and tell the thing as she saw it. Why? I don't know. I don't know. Maybe she was offered something that seemed valuable in exchange for silence. Maybe she was afraid. Maybe she thought she was above something, didn't want to get involved. Maybe she was *already* involved." I shrugged. "I don't know. But I'm going to find out."

There were some puzzled frowns.

"All I know is that I have reached through the veil."

"Well!"

"Yes!"

"I have reached through the veil, and now it's all coming on me, clear as a bell. I can see the solid thing now."

"Praise God!"

"And now, if y'all don't mind, I'd like to just be among you in a spirit of gratitude and fellowship. Y'all just saved my life, and I can't thank you enough for that."

"Don't thank us, sister! Thank the Lord!"

And then the preacher stood up and started singing "Jesus Is on the Main Line," and the music washed over me and I stood there and faked my way through the words, and clapped, and smiled, and for a little while I felt as though I had no troubles and the sun would always shine.

CHAPTER 29

AFTER THE SERVICE some people from the church helped me get a can full of gas, drove me to my Mom's Jag, and then waved cheerfully at me as I drove away. When I reached the interstate, I stopped at a pay phone and called Barrington on his cell phone.

"I need to talk to you," I said.

"Yeah," he said wearily. "We need to talk."

"I just want you to know," I said, "that I've been born again."

"In what sense?"

"Well, I'm not sure. I just feel like whatever it is that you want to say to me—and I can tell just from the tone of your voice what it is—that you need to hold off on saying it. It would be wasted to do it right now. It would be throwing away something beyond price."

There was a brief pause. "Sunny?" he said finally. "Have you been drinking?"

"No, why?"

"You sound like a bad imitation of an AME preacher."

"I'm telling you," I said. "Something changed today.

I don't know why or how, but it did. It just *did*. And whatever it is, you need to stick around to see it."

"Um. Okay, Sunny. But I have no idea what you're talking about."

I felt embarrassed suddenly. "You weren't going to tell me you wanted to break up?" I said.

"Sunny, that's another conversation. What I was going to tell you is that you've stepped in the middle of something."

"I don't follow you."

"I just got off the phone with a colleague of mine, Special Agent Stephen Mills."

"Wait, wait, wait," I said. "Mills is in the *FBI*?"

"That's what I'm telling you."

"But . . . Martha Herrington's death—that's a murder investigation. Murder's a state crime. FBI has no jurisdiction."

"That's what I'm trying to tell you, Sunny. You just stepped in the middle of some serious stink."

"Look," I said. "It doesn't matter, it doesn't matter. Like I said, I just had this really weird, life-changing experience. I'm going to drop this case, take some time off, do a little soul searching."

There was a long pause.

"No, Sunny," Barrington said. "I don't think that's going to be possible."

"What do you mean?"

"You just became a witness."

CHAPTER 30

TWO HOURS LATER I was sitting in a chair in Room 209 of the Motel 6 just off I-75 on the road to Williams County. Sitting across from me was Special Agent Stephen Mills of the FBI.

"Miss Childs," Mills was saying, "I appreciate your being here." He seemed a good deal less of an asshole than he had the previous day. So much so that I assumed the nice guy bit had to be an act.

"Yeah, well."

"Let me brief you a little bit. This is a fairly dynamic situation right now, and a good deal of it is very need-to-know. But let me bottom-line it for you. Horst and Uma Krens have been under surveillance by the Federal Bureau of Investigation for over six months. They are low-level operatives in a drug-smuggling ring involving former East German Stasi members operating both here and in Europe. This is an extremely dangerous and effective group.

"Earlier today we picked up a land line transmission on a tapped phone indicating that you had been apprehended at an undisclosed location by Karl Haupt and Werner Eigen, two higher-level members of the organization we've been working to bring down. Based upon what you've told me already, and what we learned from that tapped conversation, it is our belief that you are a potentially major witness in this case.

"I won't burden you with our operational issues, but let's put it this way: we have a great deal of general intel, but heretofore we have not had a single witness to any drug transactions conducted by this group. You are what we call a wedge witness. Your testimony will enable us to arrest and flip Uma, Karl, and Werner. They will then lead us, we believe, to even bigger fish. I can't stress how important you are to our case."

"Okay . . ." I said.

"We are offering you the following: complete protection, housing, feeding, etc., for the duration of pretrial and trial, and the opportunity to enter the witness protection program subsequent to all prosecutions."

I stared at him.

"Naturally we're prepared, if necessary, to offer certain, ah, reimbursements for lost wages, etc."

"Are you *nuts*?" I said. "Witness protection program? You're talking about my moving to another state, changing my name, never seeing my family again? Stuff like that?"

Mills cleared his throat. "Yes, ma'am. Along with, as I say, certain financial, ah, certain—"

"You must think I'm an idiot," I said.

"These people are extremely dangerous," Mills said.

I let out a long slow breath. "I need to talk to my boyfriend, Agent Cherry."

"I've spoken with Agent Cherry," he said. "He's on board with all of this."

"On board? Give me a break." I stood and started to walk toward the door.

One of Mills's henchmen in the blue windbreakers stood, blocking my way.

"Miss Childs, as I say, this is a dynamic situation."

"I don't give a damn what it is," I said. "I'm leaving."

"Miss Childs, we have prepared a material witness subpoena," Mills said, holding out a piece of paper in a blue wrapper. "We have been authorized by the Federal Court for the Northern District of Georgia to detain you for forty-eight hours."

I snatched the paper from his hand, looked at it. He wasn't kidding. A federal judge had just given the FBI authorization to make me into a prisoner of the United States government.

"I promise, Miss Childs, this is for your own safety." He gave me his best effort at a chummy smile. "As I say, the situation on the ground is very dynamic. Certain things will be resolved very shortly. And at that time, you will be free to do whatever you wish. In the meantime, I urge you to cooperate with us in the preparation of an affidavit regarding everything you witnessed in Atlanta earlier this afternoon."

"And if I refuse?"

The chummy smile faded. "I wouldn't try that if I were you."

I flopped back down on the bed. "I want to see Barrington Cherry," I said. "I want to see him right now."

Mills pulled out a cell phone, dialed a number, had a brief conversation, then closed the phone and said, "Agent Cherry will be here first thing in the morning."

•　•　•

I ate chicken fried steak, greens, and whippped potatoes with the two windbreaker guys. They were mon-
osyllabic types whose names were Decker and Brecker.

"Rhyming names," I said after we'd finished eating.
"That must be loads of fun around the office."

Decker looked at Brecker.

"Okay," I said. "Maybe not."

And that was all the conversation we had for the
next two hours. Every half hour, Decker's cell phone
would ring. He would pick it up off the bedside table
and say, "Decker." Then he would say, "Affirmative."
Then he would hang up.

At ten o'clock, I palmed Decker's phone off the table and said, "I'm going down to get a soda."

"I'll get it," Brecker said.

But I beat him to the door. "Look," I said, opening
the door. "I'm not trying to escape, okay? I'm going
to do the right thing here, I promise." I gave him the
kind of bright, flirty smile that I was sure my mother
would have used under the circumstances. "I just want
a Coke and a chance to stretch my legs."

"All right," he said grudgingly.

Brecker watched me from the doorway as I walked
down to the drink machine. When I reached the machine, I pulled out the phone I'd swiped from Agent
Decker and called my mother's cell.

"Where *are* you, darling?" she said. "I was worried
sick about you."

"Never mind," I said. "Is everything okay over
there?"

"Why wouldn't it be?"

"I want you to leave the lodge right now."

"What!"

"Just do it," I said. "Horst, Uma, and Biggs are all connected to those murders. I'm not sure how—but they know I'm on to them. You need to get out right away."

"But—"

"Now!" I snapped the phone shut, slid some quarters in the machine, and headed back to the room.

Fifteen minutes later, the phone rang. Decker picked it up and said, "Who is this? How did you get this number?" Then he frowned and handed me the phone. "It's your boyfriend."

"Barrington!" I said. "Thank God."

There was a brief pause. Then a voice tinged with a German accent said, "Actually, no. This is your friend Horst over at the lodge."

My heart sank. "How did you get this number?"

"We were monitoring your mother's cell. Biggs here is quite clever with electronic gadgetry. He tells me it's a real snap to listen in on signals from analog cell phones."

"What do you want?"

"Oh, it's not so much what *we* want. But your mother? Well, she's feeling a little under the weather right now. It really might be smart if you got over here."

"I don't—"

"Sorry, I'm being coy. I am pointing a gun at her head right now. If you don't get here in forty-five minutes, I'll kill her. If you arrive with the cops in tow, I'll kill her." He paused. "Basically what I'm saying is this: you come talk to us, work something out, we'll let her go. Otherwise, she's dead."

"I'm really not in a situation where I can—"

"Forty-five minutes or she's dead."

The phone went dead.

"Guys," I said, "you mind giving me a few minutes by myself?"

"Why?" Decker said.

I sighed. "I need to go to the bathroom."

"And?"

"Well, it's a little embarrassing, that's all."

"So shut the door."

"Could you just stand outside the room? Please, do I have to be gross about this? All that chicken fried steak is about to make my colon explode."

Brecker held up his hands in surrender. "Okay, okay. More than I needed to know."

The two agents trooped out the front door. As soon as they were gone, I rifled through my purse, pulled out my keys, dove out the back window, and started running. Fortunately they had made me park my car behind the motel so that it wouldn't be visible to any nefarious types who might be trying to hunt me down and kill me; as a result I was able to jump in my car and drive off without Decker or Brecker seeing me.

I couldn't figure out what to do. It was clear enough what Horst wanted. As soon as I got there, he'd probably kill both me and my mother. I figured I'd better think of something quick.

CHAPTER 31

UMA WAS WAITING in front of the lodge, dressed in her pale blue uniform dress and a pair of clunky white shoes.

"What happens now?" I demanded.

She looked around to make sure nobody was watching, then said softly, "Go to the shed. There's an ATV around back with a key in the ignition."

Then she turned around and walked back into the building. I went around behind the lodge, found the waiting all-terrain vehicle, and drove off into the night. I reached the shed about five minutes later. Biggs was waiting for me with a shotgun in his hand.

"I warned you twice. You should have listened."

"Yeah. Well."

"Horst is inside covering me," he said. "So don't get cutesy." He pointed at the wall with the shotgun. "Just like on TV, hands up against the wall." He kicked my feet apart then did an extremely thorough pat-down. I had a little neck knife secreted inside my bra, but he found it and threw it into the woods without comment. When he was done, I could feel his breath on my neck. "Stay calm in there and don't do anything stupid, Sunny, and everything will be all right."

"Sure," I said. My knees were weak and I didn't feel the slightest bit calm.

"In the door."

I walked through the door into the big shed. It was about a hundred feet long, with a couple of nice cars down at the far end, and a tractor by the door. As I walked around the tractor, I saw my mother. Each arm was attached to a handcuff, the other ends of which were hooked over a gambrel—the steel hooks on which deer were hung to be disemboweled—and her eyes were covered with a camouflage-colored handkerchief. Horst stood next to her, his MP-5 submachine gun pointed at her head.

"I'm here," I said. "Let her go."

"Not likely," Horst said.

"You can kill one of us, but not both," I said. Then I turned and started walking back toward the door.

"Hold on, hold on," Horst said. "I'll uncuff her, how about that? Someplace to start, yah? Establish trust, nice and slow?"

I stopped, turned. "Okay, do it."

Horst took out a key, unlocked Mom's cuffs. She slumped onto the floor. It's a disturbing thing to see somebody you've always viewed as unbendable and powerful being humiliated and abused that way.

"And the blindfold."

"I didn't say anything about the blindfold."

"The blindfold. *Now*."

He shrugged, ripped the blindfold off. My Mom's red hair was askew, but her eyes were hard. It made me feel better. She was a tough old bird.

"Okay, here it is," Horst said. "I need to know where I stand. I talked to my compatriot in Atlanta, and he said that you have figured out what we are up to here."

"Smuggling ecstasy."

"Who have you talked to? Atlanta police? FBI?"

I shook my head. "Nobody."

"Bullshit."

"I swear."

He pointed his gun at Mom's head. "Don't lie to me."

"Look," I said. "I'm a professional. Just like you. This job is just a paycheck to me."

Horst looked at me skeptically.

"My financial arrangement with the lodge, it's a kind of contingency thing. If I discover who killed these women, I get a bonus. A substantial bonus. If law enforcement solves the crime, all I get is time and expenses. Which doesn't keep me in Guccis, if you know what I mean."

Horst raised one eyebrow about a millimeter. "So?"

"So, if one more person dies here, you're burned for sure. On the other hand, if the GBI investigation doesn't turn up a killer, you and Biggs here are free to keep in business."

"GBI?" Horst said. "I thought he was FBI."

I shook my head. "No, he's GBI. FBI has no jurisdiction over murders."

"Is that true?" Horst said to Biggs.

Biggs shrugged. "I suppose so, yeah."

Horst frowned. "You're saying if I pay you sufficient money, you just walk away."

"Yep."

"What's to stop you taking my money and then telling the cops anyway?"

"Well, I'd hardly get to keep your money if I went to the cops, would I? The government would seize it as evidence."

"What about her?" Pointing to my mother.

"She'll go along with whatever I do," I said. "A hundred grand. That's the going rate for silence."

Horst laughed loudly. "Twenty-five."

"Sixty."

"All right, all right. Sixty." Horst looked thoughtful. "So you really told nobody."

"Not a soul."

Horst looked at my face for a long time, his hard eyes appraising me. I tried to look like a money-grubbing sleazeball. "You know what?" he said finally. "I believe you."

"So what was the deal?" I said. "I know you killed Martha Herrington and Jennifer Treadaway. But the thing I don't understand is why you washed their feet with bleach."

Horst gave me a look of annoyance. "I didn't kill those women."

"Who did? Biggs? Come on. You can tell me. We're partners now."

"Not really." Horst looked over at Biggs. "Go ahead and kill them now."

"Wait!" I said. "I thought we had a deal!"

"We did. I just broke it."

I felt my heart sink, not just with fear but with regret and shame. Somehow I could have done this better. Maybe by alerting Agent Mills, maybe by—well, I didn't know what else. But surely I could have done it differently. My knees went out from under me and

I began sinking to the floor. I wanted to run or fight, but my body had deserted me.

Biggs walked over to the middle bay door, pressed a big green paddle button. The bay door started slowly rising.

"What are you doing, Biggs?" Horst said.

"Don't worry," Biggs said. "I'm taking care of it."

"Kill them now," Horst said. "In here."

Biggs lifted his shotgun, pointed it at my head. And then, just as I thought it was all over, he swiveled the gun toward Horst and said, "Put the gun down, Horst."

Horst stared at Biggs. "What are you talking about?"

"Horst Krens, you are under arrest. My real name is Special Agent Doyle Farriday, I'm with the Bureau of Alcohol, Tobacco and Firearms. If you move that gun one goddamn inch, you're one seriously dead Kraut."

And then suddenly there were men swarming through the bay door and into the room, men in black body armor, with black ballistic masks over their heads, like a swarm of faceless monsters from a bad dream. "Down on the ground!" they were yelling. "Down on the ground! Down on the ground!"

Horst's face hardened, and his gun began moving upward. Then there came what seemed like an endless series of loud bangs, and Horst fell on the floor. After he went down, he didn't move at all.

CHAPTER 32

"**I THOUGHT FOR** sure I was gone," I said.

Something had changed about Biggs. His creepy look had been replaced by a slight swagger. "Touch and go there, huh?" he said. "Touch and go."

"Where's Agent Mills?" I said.

Biggs scowled. "That son of a bitch. Don't even mention his name to me."

"Wait, hold on, I don't understand."

"I've been running an undercover op for the Bureau of Alcohol, Tobacco and Firearms here for a year trying to take these people down. We were about a month away from a major bust. Top to bottom. But those jerks at the FBI decided they wanted a piece of it. So they tried to federalize the Martha Herrington murder under some bogus RICO predicate theory. Total bullshit. They were just jumping on our investigation. But once they started messing everything up, we knew we had to move, just to save what little we had. Ruined a solid year's work."

"Well, you got Uma and Horst," I said.

Biggs shook his head dismissively. "Big deal! These people were nobodies. Couriers. The big fish are two more links further up the food chain. And thanks to that pompous scum-sucking hosebag idiot moron cretin Mills, our big players are now sitting up in Atlanta, laughing their asses off. They'll probably be on planes to Europe by tomorrow morning, drinking champagne in the first-class section."

"So did Mills know that you—"

"Nope. Mills didn't even know I was an agent. He knew we had an op going down here, though. We warned him off of it, but he conned somebody in Washington, went over the head of the Atlanta multi-jurisdictional narcotics task force. And here we are." He gestured furiously down at the bleeding body of Horst Krens. "What a waste. What a ridiculous waste."

CHAPTER 33

I WENT THROUGH a weird period after that. My number one investigator at Peachtree Investigations, Tawanda Flornoy, is an Atlanta homicide cop who retired on disability after a pimp ran over her leg. Tawanda's husband is the pastor of a little church down in southwest Atlanta, much like the one that I went to after I escaped from Karl and Werner.

For about three or four months, I went down there every Sunday morning and Wednesday night, and stood in the back of the church and sang and clapped my hands, hoping to regain some sense of the peace and release I'd felt on the day I was born again—or whatever it was that had happened. And every night before bed I would read a copy of the King James Bible—not in any systematic way, but just sort of skipping around, trying to find something that I could hook my mind onto.

But after a while, I started feeling like—not precisely a fraud, but at least someone who wasn't being completely honest with herself. When I stood in the back of the little storefront church and watched everybody shouting and singing and jumping around, I felt

like, well, a witness. A witness and not a participant.
It wasn't my way of worshipping, all that emotionalism
and excitement, it just wasn't me. Plus, I still wasn't
too sure about the whole God thing—which, we must
be honest—is a fairly central part of the Christian experience, whether you go to the Episcopal Church or
the Fire Baptized Holiness Temple.

Things got better between me and Barrington,
though. More tender, more serious, more intimate. I
had made some kind of genuine breakthrough in my
life. I just still couldn't quite figure out what it was.

I found out later that Uma Krens had been arrested
at exactly the same time as Horst was shot. Her bags
were packed and ready; if Horst had given her a call
saying that I'd talked to law enforcement, she could
have been in the car and gone inside of five minutes.
The second they came through the door, I'm told, she
put her hands in the air and in a very clear, loud tone
of voice, spoke one word: "Lawyer!"

Other than that one word, they still don't know for
sure whether or not she even speaks English. Based on
my testimony and that of ATF Special Agent Doyle
Farriday—the man I'd known as Biggs—she was convicted on a trafficking charge, and received an
eight-year federal sentence. But they never pinned the
murders on her or on Horst. The FBI quickly washed
their hands of the murder investigation, handing it back
to the sheriff's office, who hot-potatoed it to the GBI,
who found insufficient evidence to charge.

I also got all prepared to testify against Karl Haupt
and Werner Eigen, who had been arrested on my testimony for kidnapping, aggravated assault, simple assault, battery, making terroristic threats, imprisonment,

use of a handgun in the commission of a felony, and
six or eight other charges which I have now forgotten.
Two days before their trial, they jumped bail and drove
across the Mexican border, never to be seen again.

Special Agent Stephen Mills was transferred to the
Fairbanks, Alaska, office of the FBI. Apparently screw-
ing up ATF investigations merits a slap on the wrist,
but only of the lightest sort: Barrington tells me that
Mills was also quietly promoted to Special Agent-in-
Charge, and jumped up to the government rank of
GS-13 or something, an automatic pay raise of almost
eighty-six hundred dollars.

Somewhere around mid-February I was having lunch
with my mother at one of the chi-chi little eateries in
Buckhead that she favors, when I told her that Barrington and I were planning to take a weekend vacation
somewhere, but that we couldn't make up our minds
where we wanted to go. I wanted beach; Barrington
wanted New York so we could see Marcus Roberts at
the Blue Note.

"Why don't you come down to the Hellespont
Lodge?" she said. "We always have a family weekend
on the last day of hunting season."

"I don't know," I said. "I'm not sure that's such a
great idea." My idea of a romantic getaway includes
neither firearms nor my mother.

But once an idea gets in Mom's head, there's no
stopping her. "Don't be silly, sweetheart. It'll be *perfect*!" Then her eyes widened and she gave me a hurt
look. "What? Oh, it's me, isn't it?"

"Mother . . ."

"I promise, sweetie." She was the wounded martyr
now. "I won't even *talk* to you."

CHAPTER 34

W E ARRIVED LATE Friday afternoon, just in time to find out that a memorial service was about to be held in the woods where Martha Herrington died. I was afraid it might be some kind of embarrassing creepy affair with black robes and chanting and goblets full of deer blood; but as it turned out, it was a nice, mannerly event.

The weather had turned unseasonably warm, the sky was blue, and a soft breeze stirred the pine trees, bringing with it a smell of impending spring. Thirty or so people standing in a semicircle in the woods at the edge of a field of clover. There was no camo in evidence. It was mostly Gore-tex and turtlenecks and tan twills, as though everyone had come out for some fly-fishing instead of a memorial service. They were an attractive bunch—husbands, wives, a couple of children—heads bowed somberly as a minister or priest in a cassock gave a brief eulogy. Martha Herrington's weeping husband read one of the Psalms, then we all threw white roses onto a pile where she'd been found, and then it was all over.

As the crowd began to disperse, I noticed GBI Agent

Wayne Allgood standing apart from the rest of the crowd, squinting in the bright sun. In his cheap blue suit, he stood out, conspicuous among all the fly-fishermen. I led Barrington over and introduced the two men. They swapped some law enforcement shop talk and then I said, "So y'all never made a case here, huh?"

Allgood shook his head.

"I guess Horst took the whole thing to his grave," I said.

Allgood looked at me curiously. "You really think so?"

"What do you mean?"

"I mean, do you really think it was Horst Krens who did this?"

"Sure. Who else could it have been? One of *these* people?" I waved my hand at the attractive, self-confident crowd.

"Why not?" he said sharply. "Rich folks are about as bloodthirsty as anybody else." The wind stirred his polyester tie. I wondered if it wasn't some kind of class envy talking.

Martha's husband approached us. He was a slightly stooped, earnest-looking man of about fifty, with a tennis player's tan. "Dale Herrington," he said, shaking my hand. "Sunny, Agent Allgood says you put yourself in harm's way trying to find out who killed my wife. I never got a chance to thank you."

"Part of the job," I said lamely.

"No, ma'am," he said. "There's no job that should ask that kind of sacrifice of a person. So if there's anything I can do for you, you just call me." He handed me a card. "That line goes straight to me."

I nodded. "She ever give you the impression that she was in any kind of trouble before she died, Mr. Herrington?" I said.

"Trouble?"

"I don't know—excited, nervous, worried."

Dale Herrington smiled a little. "She was a fairly strong personality, if you know what I mean. She was always going on about something."

"And before her murder?"

He looked up at the blue sky. "Yes," he said finally. "Yes, I think she was worried about something. I assume she had found out about these criminals and wasn't quite sure how to handle it."

"But she never said."

"No. She never said."

"Have you given any thought about the bleach on the feet?" I said. "Did that mean anything to you?"

Dale Herrington IV squinted at me. "The what?"

"Both she and Jennifer Treadaway were discovered barefoot, and their feet had been cleaned with bleach."

Dale Herrington kept looking at me with the same curious expression.

Agent Allgood somewhat hastily jumped in: "Ah, Sunny, Mr. Herrington had sort of requested that I not give him too many details regarding the condition of the deceased when she was found. Kind of wanted to keep it broadbrush, see?"

Herrington turned to the GBI agent. "This is true, Agent Allgood? About the bleach on the feet?"

"Yes, sir."

"Did you handle both cases?"

"Yes, sir."

"Well, now you've got me curious. What's your

speculation about why Horst would have washed their feet off?"

Allgood looked uncomfortable. "I got to be honest, sir, I really never was able to figure it out."

Herrington nodded thoughtfully, then shook hands all around and walked slowly away.

CHAPTER 35

O N **MONDAY MORNING** I arrived late to the office and found a FedEx package waiting on my desk. Inside was a check drawn on the account of Herrington Products International, and a letter printed on the most expensive-looking paper I'd seen in my life.

The letter was brief and to the point. It said,

Dear Ms. Childs:

Please accept this check in the amount of $10,000. I was troubled by our conversation. Therefore, I wish to offer you another check in the same amount upon receipt of a satisfactory explanation as regards the bleached feet. If you require further funds for expenses, etc., please contact my assistant, Mr. Dennison, at this office.

I have spoken to Governor Barnes, who has assured me that the GBI will offer you any necessary assistance in this matter.

Best regards,
Dale Herrington, IV
Chairman, Herrington Products
International, Inc.

I put in a call to Wayne Allgood at the GBI.

"Friends in high places, huh?" he said. "My boss got a call from his boss—who apparently got a call from the governor himself."

"So I assume you wouldn't have a problem messengering up a copy of the case file?"

Allgood sighed wearily. "Any friend of the gov is a friend of mine."

"In fact, let me get the files on both Herrington *and* Treadaway."

"Okey-dokey," he said.

Three hours later, a state patrolman walked in the door of my office, dropped a box on my desk, and walked out without speaking. Inside were all the case files. I closed the door and spent the rest of the day reading and taking notes.

When I was done, I wrote a list of names—all the people who had been at the lodge on the days of both murders. My mother's name was at the top. It was followed by nine others.

Bonnie Hathaway	Member
Elise Shore	Member
Robin Vandecourt	Member
Rose Ellen Knight	Member
Emily Stubbins	Member
Agent Doyle Farriday	Law Enforcement Officer
Alf Goode	Employee
Jimmy Lawford	Employee
Horst Krens	Employee
Uma Krens	Employee

I called the number that Dale Herrington IV had given me, got his assistant, Mr. Dennison, who grudgingly passed me on to His Eminence.

"Sunny," he said warmly. "How are you?"

"I got the material you asked for," I said. "I've got an angle I'd like to pursue. But to do so, I'll need to know how much pull you have in this town."

"I have some friends," he said modestly.

I told him what I needed.

When I was finished with my explanation, he said, "I'll make some calls."

An hour later my phone rang. "Good morning, Ms. Childs," a raspy voice said. "This is Charles Osgood, how are you this afternoon?"

"I'm well, General," I said. "Very kind of you to call me." Charles T. Osgood was the attorney general of the state.

"Mr. Herrington has explained what he's interested in. Now, I have to tell you that matter is not under my direct jurisdiction."

"However . . ."

"However, if you were to meet with the district attorney of Williams County, I would be glad to send my top assistant, Debra Ann Dupree, to the meeting, where she would express my strongest support for your plan."

"Is she persuasive?" I said.

Charles T. Osgood just laughed.

The next morning I walked into the Williams County Courthouse, accompanied by a tall, leggy, extremely beautiful black woman wearing a suit which managed to give an impression of conservatism, while leaving no curve of her body unrevealed.

The district attorney of Williams County was a short, very dark-skinned man named Harvard Reece. He seemed so dumbstruck by Debra Ann Dupree, who spoke not a single word during the entire meeting, that I was afraid he wasn't even listening to me. The lawyer from the attorney general's office just sat there, radiating raw female heat, and Harvard Reece just stared at her.

When I was done making my pitch, I said, "Mr. Reece?"

He looked at me as though surprised. "Yes?"

"So? What do you think?" I had been worried that he would reject the idea outright.

He frowned.

"I think Ms. Dupree's presence here speaks very clearly about the attorney general's support of this plan," I added.

His gaze flicked back to her hemline. "Ah. What would I need to do?"

At that point Debra Ann Dupree leaned forward, slid a document across the table, and with one long red fingernail, pointed at the place she wanted him to sign. He nearly stabbed himself getting the pen out of his pocket.

After the meeting was over, and we were back in Debra Ann Dupree's state-owned Ford, I said, "Is it always like that?"

She shrugged, as though intensely bored by the whole subject of her vast powers over men. "Mostly."

"So," I said, "you feel like a trip to women's prison?"

CHAPTER 36

ACCORDING TO THE plastic sign posted at the gate of the Atlanta Women's Penitentiary, visitors were not allowed on Tuesdays. But that didn't seem to include personal emissaries of the attorney general of Georgia. The warden himself came out to greet us. He was a red-faced, big-shouldered man of fifty or so, with a country boy air about him.

He took us into his office and chatted amiably about Georgia politics for a great long while—mostly with Debra Ann Dupree, since I know more about cellular biology than I do Georgia politics. Like the DA of Williams County, he seemed to have a high degree of interest in Debra Ann Dupree's hemline. Finally, with great reluctance, he dialed somebody on the phone and said, "You got the prisoner ready?" Then he set the phone down. "We got her in our finest interview room." Then he winked at Debra Ann. I might as well have been furniture.

Uma Krens was waiting for us in a small room with flaking cinderblock walls and a steel door, both of which appeared to have been painted about fifty times since the place was constructed. Uma's white prison jumpsuit made her look even paler and blonder than before. She looked up at us, head cocked, bored.

"Miss Krens, my name is Ms. Dupree," the lawyer from the attorney general's office said, "and I'm here to tell you that today is your lucky day."

Uma Krens looked at her impassively with her blue-white eyes.

"As you know, charges have not yet been made in the murders of Jennifer Treadaway and Martha Herrington. We have good reason to believe that you are connected with both of those murders. If your brother committed those murders and law enforcement is able to prove that you had knowledge of them, you are potentially liable for the death penalty. Do you understand this?"

Uma didn't move.

"Uma, do you speak English?"

"Yeah. I speak English." She had a strong accent, stronger than her brother.

"See, when you're part of a criminal enterprise and you have knowledge before or after the fact of a murder which is committed as part of a felony or felonious enterprise in which you participated, you can be prosecuted just the same as if you had done the deed. That's black letter law."

"Get to the point."

"The GBI has continued to pursue the cases. They are closer to solving these cases than they were a year ago."

"Bullshit. Otherwise you wouldn't be here."

"Here's the deal. Eight years from now, you are a free woman. But if we walk out that door, then at any moment for the rest of your life, someone can come up behind you and say, 'Uma Krens, you are under arrest for the murders of Jennifer Treadaway and Martha Herrington.' Even though you didn't commit them. There's no statute of limitation on murder." Debra Ann took the paper she'd gotten Harvard Reece to sign, slid it across the table. "What this is, is an offer of transactional immunity. If you tell us everything you know about those two murders, and do so without any deception, the district attorney of Williams County, with the full authority of the attorney general of the State of Georgia, is prepared to offer you immunity from any further prosecution on those charges."

Uma suddenly looked interested. "You say, I sign this, no possible charge for this crime? Not ever?"

"Exactly. All you have to do is sign here."

Uma studied the paper. "I need a lawyer to advise on this."

I stood, opened the door. Standing in the door was the lawyer who had represented Uma in her federal trial, Mike Friend, a top criminal attorney in Atlanta. When Dale Herrington IV says, "Make it so," things tend to go smoothly.

Uma looked a little surprised. "You people go to a lot of trouble. Maybe this too easy."

Mike Friend sat down and said, "Hi, Uma." He was an ugly, chubby little guy with a tuft of beard under his lip and a smarmy manner. But he was a good lawyer. "First, I must disclose to you that my fee has been paid by Dale Herrington, the husband of Martha Herrington. Nevertheless, that fee has already been paid and there are no strings attached. I am your lawyer, working exclusively for your interests. If you wish to retain another lawyer, that's up to you. Now your question as I walked in here is a legitimate one. My understanding is that Mr. Herrington wants some closure here. He wants to know what happened to his wife. He's a very powerful and influential guy and he's willing to use that influence to nullify these potential charges against you, if that will give him what he wants. It seems that the law enforcement authorities involved are willing to go along with his wishes. That said, I've reviewed this document already, Uma. It's quite a good deal for you. Assuming you tell the truth, you walk away from this whole mess."

Uma narrowed her eyes slightly. "I want federal charges reduced."

"Not possible," Debra Ann Dupree said.

Uma shrugged. "Then I'm going back to my needlepoint class. I'm doing a nice sampler. It says: *Home Sweet Home.* Soon I put it up on the wall."

"Hold on, hold on," Mike Friend said. "What about transfer to a minimum security facility? The federal camp over in Alabama maybe? No lockdowns, good recreational facilities, and a much nicer class of clientele."

Uma looked at me, raised her eyebrows questioningly. I looked at the assistant attorney general. Debra Ann pulled out a cell phone, had a brief conversation, then hung up.

"Done," she said.

"No possible charges on murder, transfer to federal camp in Alabama?" Uma said.

Debra Ann nodded.

Uma looked at Mike Friend, who shrugged. "It's a good deal, Uma."

Uma leaned forward and signed the document.

I put a pocket recorder on the table. "Let's start with Jennifer Treadaway. Tell us everything you know."

Uma's lip curled. "Whore. All those women at lodge, they act like queens of the world, but I know the truth about them all. Jennifer Treadaway, she start out a truckstop whore, work her way up to marrying rich guy. But in her heart . . ." Uma tapped the middle of her own chest. ". . . she still nothing but whore."

"You could probably skip the editorializing," I said. "What actually *happened*?"

Uma's pale blue eyes met mine. I don't think I'd ever seen such cold eyes on a woman. "Jennifer Treadaway, her husband got in difficult financials several years ago. At such time, she begin blackmail several members of Hellespont Lodge. Fine. Who cares. Not my problem. But then, as is matter of public record, I and my brother is engage in alleged illegal narcotic activities. Of course, these is false charges with regards to me personally." She smiled a little.

"I will be frank with you. My brother Horst, he's a very bad man. I hate to speak ill of dead, but this is fact. He is trafficker of narcotics. I admit this, right here. Any involvement I had, I maintain now and forever, is because I am unwilling dupe and plus he force me." She smiled again, having fun with us. "But nevertheless, it is fact that light plane land periodically at Hellespont Lodge, bringing shipment of product from Amsterdam by way of Mexico or various Carribbean nation. Okay? This is matter of public record.

"So how Mrs. Jennifer Treadaway connected? Total accident. Mrs. Treadaway, one time she shoot this deer. She not very good shot, because she lackadaisical, careless personality. Deer wound but not dead. Deer go running through woods, all bleeding on leaves and everything. She follow trail of deer blood. Deer run out onto runway while Horst unloading product. Crazy deer actually run into airplane, bang, somehow part of product drop on ground, due to surprise or something. Anyway Mrs. Jennifer Treadaway, she coming behind this deer, she pick up product that have fall on runway.

"She take product back to room, lo and behold, is drug material secretly hide in jar of peanut butter. So she spy on Horst. She make various incriminating videotape, certain audio recording, certain observation, so on so on so on. Then she take material to Horst, say, 'Horst, now you give ten thousand dollar to me.'

"Horst say, 'Okay.' Better to pay. But then she come back and she come back, soon payment become burdensome. She live very high lifestyle, no self-control. She begin also using product from Horst. Ecstasy, coke, blotter, various product. Finally one night she approach Horst, ask for more money. She drinking, taking marijuana, she very unreasonable, wearing little shiftless nightgown, revealing all her body parts. Is disgraceful. Horst say, 'Okay, no money, but here, you take these various product.' Like I say—coke, ecstasy, certain other drugs. She say, 'No, I take money. Only money.' Horst say, 'Not possible. You take drugs or you get nothing.'

"I'm sure I don't see this or be aware of it, of course, but later I hear about." She seemed to find this amusing, pretending she hadn't actually witnessed the crime. "But anyway, she slap container of product, knock it out of Horst's hand, all type of illegal stuffs go on the floor. Very much product on floor. Horst, at this time, he get pissed, he hit her. Very hard. She get scared, run away. Horst, he see handwriting on wall, this not gonna work out so good. He pursue down hallway, he grab her by mouth and maybe also throat to make silence. Maybe also stick knife in her neck. Next thing you know, she dead. He drop her on the floor. But as soon as she hit ground, he see her feet all cover with powder. Drugs from floor, see.

"Now, Horst, he not stupid. He know that autopsy going to discover drug residue on feet. So he—" She looked at Mike Friend. "No matter what I did, no possibility of jail?"

"No possibility."

"Okay. Okay. Horst get me, he say clean feet, clean hallway, clean floor. Better be damn clean, too, right. So I get solvent call PERC—name short for perethelene chloride, something like this—clean feet off with it. PERC, very good solvent, use in manufacture of cocaine. Problem is, now Jennifer Treadaway, her feet, they smell like PERC. Very strong, very unusual smell. So I clean feet with bleach to remove this odor. Now feet smell like bleach, so I say to hell with it, I give up."

"And that was it?" I said.

"Yeah. That's the whole story, why feet smell like bleach."

"Okay, what about Martha Herrington? She's the one I came for."

Uma grinned at me. "Sad for you, you go to all this trouble then."

I frowned. "What are you talking about!"

She laughed loudly. "I'm afraid I outfox yourself. You give me immunity for both crime, so you find out about Mrs. Herrington. Problem is, I don't know diddly about why Mrs. Herrington die."

"But—"

"I tell you straight up, Miss Childs. I don't know nothing about no Mrs. Herrington."

My face went hard. "You're lying."

Uma sat back slowly in her chair, crossed her powerful arms across her chest, and looked at me with obvious amusement.

"Okay, so maybe Horst did it without telling you."

She shook her head. "No. It wasn't Horst."

"How do you know?"

"I was with Horst."

"When?"

"Until nine o'clock in the morning. At nine o'clock he go out with Biggs. The ATF guy. So Biggs account for his whereabout after that, give sworn deposition. I don't like Biggs, but I don't see no reason he lie in this matter."

"Hold on, hold on. Explain to me *exactly* when you were with Horst."

"That's what I'm saying. I'm with him all night."

"In the same, what, in the same apartment?"

There was a long silence. Uma met my eye, gave me a look. "In the same bed."

More silence.

"Fuck all of you," she said. "I have special understanding of Horst. He have special needs, which I understand, fuck all of you."

"Special needs?" I said softly.

She gave me a sly look, then leaned back in her chair, let her head loll back, and her eyes rolled into her head. However pale her skin was to start with, it became even paler. She looked like a dead woman. Which brought back my conversation with Rose Ellen Knight, who said that in her experience Horst liked a woman to play dead in bed.

"I don't understand what you're doing," Debra Ann Dupree said. "Is this some kind of creepy demonstration?"

"Trust me, you don't want to know," I said. "Suffice it to say, I feel fairly confident she's not lying in this particular instance. She probably was with her brother."

"Was it *you*, then, Miss Krens?" the assistant attorney general asked. "Did you kill Martha Herrington?"

Uma sat up quickly, regaining her color. "No."

"We can still rescind this agreement," I said.

"You can't do that," Mike Friend said.

"We can if she's lying," Debra Ann Dupree snapped.

"I'm not lying," Uma said. "According to agreement, even if I kill her, I can't get prosecute, right?"

"That's right," Mike Friend said.

"So I got no incentage to lie, huh? If I kill her, I tell you. But I didn't kill her."

The room was silent for a long time.

"Look," Uma said. "I use bleach for specific purpose. Cocaine on feet, PERC clean cocaine, bleach clean PERC. Even if I kill Mrs. Herrington, what the odds I'm going to have to do bleach twice?"

"So Martha Herrington didn't know you had a drug thing going here at all?"

"No."

"She wasn't blackmailing you or threatening you?"

"I tell you. I got no knowledge why she killed."

It was my turn to slump back in my chair. "But . . ."

I said. And that was all that I could think to say.

"What you looking at," Uma said confidently, "you looking at copycat crime."

"Oh, give me a break."

Uma seemed offended. "You watch TV, read news? Copycat crime happen all the time. Those kid in Colorado, go into school shoot all their friends? They see this in a movie, some kid in a black trenchcoat kill everybody, so they wear black trenchcoat, go in, do same thing. Not even original idea." Uma stood. "I sign this agreement. I enter in good faith. You try to take away, my lawyer tear you a new asshole in court of law."

Was she torturing us? Maybe she committed the second murder herself and was afraid if she admitted it, we'd find some loophole in the agreement and prosecute her for it. Or maybe, simplest-case scenario, she was telling the truth.

"Copycat killer," she said. Then she banged on the door. "Guard! Hello, boss! I got to go to needlepoint!"

CHAPTER 37

So NOW WE knew the truth about Jennifer Treadaway. But that left me no closer to what had happened to Martha Herrington.

I brought the box containing the files on the two cases home with me that night and put it in the middle of my kitchen table. Before I got involved with Barrington, I'd eaten off a card table. But Barrington is not quite as Spartan as I am, so when we had moved in together, his expensive furniture had come with him. The kitchen table with seating for ten turned out to make a great work space. Barrington is constantly clearing all my stuff off of it and putting it someplace. But that's one of those little things that happens in a relationship. I used to get mad at him when he lost "important" bits of paper and scribbles I'd left on the table. But now I just let it go. We'd gone through a bad patch and now things were looking better. No point getting tripped up over stupid little things.

"What you got?" Barrington said, pouring us both some wine. He had been on a stakeout the night before, so I hadn't had a chance to tell him about the case coming back to life.

I took out one set of files, set them down at one end of the huge table. "Here, Treadaway." I took out another set of files, set them at the other end. "Here, Herrington."

"I thought that case was long gone."

"It rose from the dead." I told him the whole story, ending by giving him a blow by blow of the interview with Uma Krens.

"So, assuming she's not lying, that narrows it down to who?"

"Well, that's the problem. Originally I was going on the single-perp theory. Which meant I could narrow it down to the people who were there both times. But now . . ." I sighed. "Now I'm back to having to look at everybody who was there the day she was killed."

"How many people was that?"

"I think there were about twenty club members there."

"And of those, how many could be expected to know where she was?"

"Probably only a handful."

"There you are, then."

"The ATF agent, Biggs—that's not his real name, but that's how I think of him—he knew. And according to his witness statement, he told Horst. It was Horst's job to always keep track of which stands the members were in. So Uma might have known, too. Plus four members of the lodge came along when she was delivered to her stand: Elise Shore, Robin Vandecourt, Rose Ellen Knight, and Emily Stubbins."

"You rule out Biggs, Horst, and Uma, you got four names."

"You're smart, Barrington," I said. "You ought to be in the FBI or something."

We laughed and then I cracked the first file and began reading.

CHAPTER 38

THE NEXT MORNING I arrived at the sociology building at Emory University at around ten o'clock. The door with EMILY STUBBINS, PHD written on it was wide open. Emily herself was talking to a whiny young kid with a ring through his eyebrow. He was complaining that the grade she'd given him was going to ruin his chances for medical school. "Then you should have written a better paper," she said brightly. "Anything else?"

The kid glared at her. "This isn't fair."

"Sure it is."

"Well, don't be surprised if you hear from my dad," he hissed. "His best friend in the world is on the board of directors."

"Yes, young man, and as you're probably aware, my husband is president of the university. Now please get out of my office before I get tired of maintaining my usual cheerful demeanor."

The glowering boy slouched down the hallway, muttering ugly little mysogynisms.

"Oh, Sunny!" Emily waved at me, smiling broadly. "Come on in." I entered and she said, "Close the door.

Even us female profs are afraid to close doors on our students nowadays. Sexual harassment."

"Thanks," I said, sitting. "I appreciate your seeing me at such short notice."

"Oh, God, don't mention it. The life of a professor is so stultifying you wouldn't believe. You bring a little excitement. What's going on? No more dead bodies, I trust?"

"Well, the same dead bodies actually."

She frowned, puzzled. "I thought they'd decided it was that Horst person."

"One of them was. Jennifer Treadaway. But Martha Herrington is still unsolved."

"Oh."

"The reason I came to you is that I remember you saying something that struck me at the time as kind of funny. But now that I think back. Well . . . my point is, I think you might be able to help me."

"Whatever I can do."

"Okay. Here's the thing. When I first started my investigation, I quickly determined that Jennifer Treadaway was blackmailing several members of the club. Turned out, of course, that didn't have anything directly to do with why she was killed. I'm shortcutting the story—which I know now in some detail—but she got involved with Horst and the drug thing. Ultimately that led to her death."

"I see."

"Uma Krens confessed to her part in Jennifer's murder. There was drug residue of some sort on her feet when Horst killed her and Uma cleaned her feet with solvent and bleach to get the residue off. All well and good. But Uma—who was given immunity from prosecution—claims she had nothing to do with Martha Herrington's murder. She says it wasn't Horst either."

"You think she's telling the truth?"

"My gut instinct says yes."

She licked her lips. "So . . . I'm a suspect? Is that why you're here?"

"Not really," I said. "I was more looking for some advice."

"Oh," she said. "You had me worried for a minute there." Then she laughed her big booming laugh.

"Like I say, my original theory of the crime was blackmail. But then the drug thing came along. Now the drug theory seems not to apply to Martha. So I'm back to square one. And that was when something came back to me. We had an interesting discussion, remember? About the women in the lodge? And you said, never get between a woman and her intended mate."

"Did I? It sounds awfully glib."

I laughed. "Maybe so. But what I'm getting at is, what *would* make one of those women kill one of their friends? Maybe it was a dispute over a man or something. I don't know. You're a trained observer of people and their behavior. So basically, I was hoping you might have some theories."

"Okay."

"Maybe you heard some gossip, observed a fight, found out about some dispute that Martha had with any of the other women. Anything . . ."

She rested her big solid head on her big solid hands, and looked off into the distance. "You know?" she said finally. "Something does come to mind."

"What?"

She frowned. "I mean, this is probably nothing."

"Look, I know that you're probably uncomfortable saying something that might imply somebody was guilty of . . . hurting Martha. But I promise I'm not going to jump to conclusions."

"Okay. Here it is. The day before the murder, I saw Martha Herrington fighting with another member of the club. I mean it was a very, ah, a very intense-looking argument. Martha had tears running down her face and stuff."

"Who? Who was it?"

"Elise Shore."

I thought about it for a moment. "Martha Herrington was, what, close to six feet tall? And Elise Shore is about my size. Maybe even smaller. I can't really see a tiny woman like Elise killing somebody as big as Martha."

"Like I say, I don't think it meant anything. I'm just telling you what I saw."

I nodded. "I'm curious about one other thing. You said you saw Biggs follow Martha Herrington, then he came back and threw something into the woods."

She raised her eyebrows. "Did I?"

"Yes, you did."

"Whew. It's been a long time." She looked thoughtful. "Yeah, now that you mention it, I remember."

"But he definitely threw something."

"Yeah."

"Where did he throw it?"

She furrowed her brow. "Gosh. I'd really be hard pressed to say. He was standing behind the big garage shed, next to the smaller tool shed kind of thing. And he just kind of chunked it. Off into the woods."

"Straight back into the pines."

"I'm a little hazy, honestly."

"Could you see what he threw?"

"No."

"Big thing? Little thing?"

She shrugged. "Yay big, maybe." She held her hands about ten inches apart.

"The size of a knife."

Emily Stubbins squinted at me curiously. "You're not saying . . . I mean he's a cop."

"I'm just talking."

CHAPTER 39

I CALLED THE Atlanta office of the ATF, but according to the agent I talked to, Biggs—Special Agent Doyle Farriday, that is—was on special assignment and wouldn't be available for several days.

So I called my mother and asked if she knew where I could get hold of Elise Shore. "Why, she's coming over this afternoon for a little bridge club thing I'm throwing."

"Wouldn't some *other* time be better, dear?" Mom said when she saw her maid leading me into the house. I could see that she was furious at me for crashing her little party. But naturally she had to give me the big MMMOOOAAHH! MMMOOOOAAAHH! on the cheeks and pretend like she was glad to see me.

"Now's going to have to do," I said.

Then I plowed through the knot of ladies in the back yard. They all seemed to be wearing butterscotch. I guess it was the year of butterscotch for rich ladies of a certain age in Atlanta. I was the only woman at the bridge club thing who was wearing black. Also the only woman wearing cowboy boots. Growing up, I had always been the girl wearing butterscotch when everybody else had seen the smoke signals saying they were supposed to be wearing pastels. Thank God for black. Now I'm always dressed the wrong color and I don't care.

Elise Shore was talking to an old woman who had obviously just gotten a face-lift, her eyebrows stretched up so tight that she looked like she was stuck in a perpetual state of surprise.

"You don't mind if I steal Mrs. Shore from you for a moment, do you?"

The woman looked at me with her surprised face, and said, "Honey, I just *love* that outfit. I would never have the *courage*!"

I managed to pry Elise Shore away from the surprised woman. She looked about as happy to see me as my mother. "Well, my gracious, what a surprise to see you, Sunny."

"This will be quick, I promise."

"Oh, don't think a thing about it." She smiled her little paste-on smile, and batted her eyes. "It's just a boring old garden party."

"There's something I need to ask you about that morning when Martha Herrington was killed."

"I thought that crime had long ago been solved," she said, still with the paste-on smile.

"No," I said. "It hasn't."

She cocked her head a little, blinked, waited.

"I was looking at all the witness statements this morning. Everybody who went out on the tram with Martha Herrington made a statement to that FBI agent, Mills. I've been reviewing those statements, and I've found some inconsistencies. Not in the statements themselves, but between what certain people told me, and what they told the FBI."

Her smiled faltered a little. "Could we, perhaps, do this another time, dear? These are my *friends*."

"No," I said. "I think we need to do this now."

She breathed in, then out, then in again. Then finally she said, "All right, dear, let's go inside, shall we? It's just sweltering out here."

We went into my mother's formal parlor. Apparently butterscotch was the interior color of choice this year, too. Elise Shore sat on the overstuffed couch, her handbag and her shoes matching perfectly with the throw pillows and the Hindustani rug.

"What order did everybody get off the tram?"

Elise Shore looked at me with a flat, distant gaze. "Honey, let's get this straight. It's been several months and I don't remember."

"In your statement to the FBI, you said that you were the last one to get off the tram, other than Martha Herrington."

"Then I guess it's true."

"Also you said in your witness statement that after you climbed up the ladder into your hunting stand, you saw somebody on an ATV drive past."

"Then I must have."

"When I asked you about that morning, you never mentioned anybody on an ATV."

She looked out the window. "That Agent Mills person was very rude. He kept asking the same things over and over and over. I suppose he may have gotten a detail or two out of me that I forgot to mention to you."

"So this person on the ATV—you saw them clearly?"

"Clear enough."

"In your statement you identified this person. Are you absolutely sure?"

"Three months is a long time to remember some little bitty old thing like that."

"So you remember or you don't?"

Elise looked at me nervously. "Why are you doing this, Sunny?"

I stared at her. "I think you know. You had a fight with Martha Herrington the day before she was murdered."

"I'm not one to fly off the handle ordinarily," she said, looking at me with a flat stare. "But as you have gone to so much trouble to find out, I am capable of expressing anger when pressed hard enough."

"And Martha Herrington pressed you hard enough."

"Not *that* hard. If you're implying I snuck up there and killed her."

"I'm not implying anything. I just want to know what the two of you had a fight about."

"It's none of your business."

"It would sure be a shame if it leaked out to all your garden club friends that you'd burned your first husband to death."

Elise Shore met my eyes for a long time. "You enjoy this, don't you?" she said. "Sitting in judgment."

"No. But I guess I do enjoy finding the truth."

She snorted. "The truth. Truth, in my experience, is a pale substitute for compassion."

"What did you argue about, Mrs. Shore?"

"That woman was a predator," she said finally. "She used people. She used men. Not to get things—she was well beyond needing anything from men—but just because she could, because she liked destroying things. She'd done ugly things with husbands of several of the ladies at the lodge."

"How do you know this?"

"I just do."

"And, what, she seduced your husband, too?"

"My husband?" She laughed bitterly. "Oh, no. That I could have lived with."

"Then who."

She looked away for a moment. "With my son. He's seventeen years old."

"How did you find out?"

When she told me the answer, I frowned. There was something here that I was missing. But I just couldn't figure out quite what it was.

"If we're done here, darling, I really should get back to the group," Elise Shore said, picking up her butterscotch handbag. "People will wonder."

"Let me ask you a question," I said. "How do you know that this year it's butterscotch?"

She cocked her head and looked at me curiously. "Sunny," she said, "there is something very peculiar about you, but I just can't put my finger on what it is."

CHAPTER 40

WENT BACK to the office, read over the notes I'd taken during the course of my investigation. Then I compared my notes with the witness statements taken by Agent Mills. The differences I found in the stories were small but significant. And they didn't seem to add up to a pattern of mistakes. These were lies. They had to be.

I arrived in Hightower, Georgia, the next morning just in time to get stuck in what passes for a traffic jam in that part of the world. It was a funeral. Three cars full of sheriff's deputies crawled by, blue lights flashing, preceded the old black hearse, which in turn preceded what must have been a hundred and fifty or two hundred cars, all of them with their headlights lit. It went on and on and on, the cars crawling by at about ten miles an hour. It is the custom in rural Georgia to stop dead in the road when a funeral passes by, so there I was, stuck between a pickup truck and a tractor towing a hay bailer, drumming my fingers on the steering wheel with ever-increasing irritation. It was only when the last car passed and I recognized the face inside,

that it occurred to me who must have died. Two deputies on Harleys, blue lights flashing, took up the rear.
As they passed, I hung a U-turn in the middle of the
desolate strip of road and followed the procession.

The graveyard was a beautiful old spot, with two
entrances in the stone wall which surrounded it. You
could still see the ghostly impression in the rock next
to the smaller gate where they'd removed the letters
that said COLORED ENTRANCE.   I parked, and walked
out to the spot where they were burying the late Sheriff
Teddy T. Timmers. The live oak trees were ancient and
gnarled, and the graveyard was full of old, worn, but
still extravagant monuments—worn and cracked mon-
oliths, cherubs weeping limestone tears, Doric col-
umns, alabaster-clad mausoleums—that were the only
remaining sign of Williams County's former grandeur
and wealth.

Old habits die hard. I noticed all the black folks
stood on one side of the grave, all the whites on the
other. There was a muted, but decidedly festive un-
dercurrent among the blacks, and a wistful, gloomy
look among the whites. I don't suppose anybody
missed Sheriff Timmers on any personal level—but he
represented the passing of an age that would never return.

After the ceremony was over, I found Rochelle Longineau climbing into Sheriff Timmer's official Lincoln
with the star on the side.

She raised her eyebrows slightly. "Ms. Childs," she
said. "Pleasure to see you again."

"You have any plans for the afternoon?" I said.

"I was thinking about maybe getting fitted for a new
uniform," she said.

"Should I call you *Sheriff* Longineau?" I said.

"Oh, it'll be a couple weeks before it's official," she said. "Timmers' poor fool of a son thinks he's taking over for the old man." She smiled slightly. "I'll need to get together with him and explain some things."

"Look," I said, "I was wondering if I could borrow some of your men this afternoon."

"Hop in," she said. "Let's talk in the car."

An hour later I was out at the Hellespont Lodge. The place had a deserted feel. Hunting season was over, so there were no members staying there. Mom told me they had found a part-time groundskeeper, but Horst and Uma hadn't yet been permanently replaced, so things were getting a little overgrown.

I led Sheriff-to-be Longineau and six of her men, all of them still wearing their dress uniforms, complete with patent leather Sam Brown belts and gleaming knee-high boots, down to the shed.

"So what exactly do you think we're looking for?" Rochelle Longineau said.

"I don't know. Possibly a knife."

"Where do you want to start?"

"According to Emily Stubbins's statement, he threw whatever it was into the woods." I got out of the Lincoln, stood with my back to the weedy field that bordered the shed. "So I guess we just start here and work a grid."

Rochelle Longineau nodded. "Fellows," she said. "You heard the lady. Form a line, please, eight feet apart, and work your line through the woods about fifty yards. When you get done with that, come back to the

path, we'll shift the whole line over and start the process again. Questions?"

The sun was dead in the middle of the sky as we
began the search. The month of May had taken a
turn—as it often does in Georgia—toward the tropical.
Within an hour, the men were grumbling and complaining, the sweat staining their uniforms, their crisp
linen gone soggy, their faces streaming with sweat.

We kept on until two o'clock, when Rochelle
brought us lunch from Williams County's one restau-
rant. Think deep fried.

Then we were back to it again. All the soul food
had me wishing for a nice siesta, but I figured I'd better
keep at it or the deputies were liable to walk off the
job en masse.

The sun started slipping down toward the horizon as
we worked a fan-shaped pattern that Rochelle had laid
out with a red pen on a topographical map she kept on
the hood of the Lincoln. It was just getting dark when
we finished working the last pie-shaped section on the
map.

"Nothing?" she said.

I shook my head wearily. "I don't get it."

She stood there and looked out at the woods. "Deputy Morris," she said to a tall young black man.

"Yes, ma'am."

"If you were standing here and you wanted to throw
something into the woods, where would you throw it?"

The young deputy scanned the woods, pointed his
finger. "Probably over yonder."

She opened up the glove compartment of the Lincoln, took out a sheath knife, and tossed it to him.
"Here. Throw it."

The deputy wound up, heaved it into the woods.

"All right, gentlemen," Rochelle said. "Go find that knife. Then start working your way out in a circle. And however hard you looked the first time, be twice as careful now."

One of the white deputies mumbled something under his breath.

"*Excuse* me?" Rochelle Longineau snapped.

The deputy looked away sullenly.

"Look," I said. "Maybe it's just not—"

"Miss Childs," Rochelle Longineau said. "As of right now, this is *my* investigation. When I tell my people to get to work, they best hop to it." She glared around the semicircle of sullen, sweaty faces. She clapped her hands. "Now!"

The deputies began trooping into the woods.

They found the knife the deputy had thrown in less than five minutes, formed up, and began working their way slowly outward. After a few minutes I went back to the car to get a drink of water.

"I didn't mean to jump down your throat," Rochelle said. "But I got to whip these boys into shape from day one. If they get the impression they can question my resolve, then I might as well quit."

"No problem," I said.

The sun got down into the trees and it started getting hard to see. Flashlights appeared, the beams of light moving around in the woods like wraiths among the trees. Finally Rochelle called out, "All right, boys. Time to saddle up."

I came out of the woods and shook my head. "I'm sorry," I said. "This was a big waste of time."

"Don't apologize. This was a useful exercise."

"Seriously, I feel stupid."

"A witness told you something, we attempted to ver-
ify their statement. That doesn't mean we failed."

I thought about what she said, while the deputies got
back in their cars.

"We'll wait until they're all gone," she said, "then
I'll take you back to your car."

"Sure."

She watched the cars drive away, leaned up against
the Lincoln in her white nurse's uniform. "I got to be
the first one in and the last one out," she said. Then
she began weeping.

"It's lonely at the top," I said.

She smiled a little, wiped her eyes. "No, it's not
that." She paused, stared out into the darkness. "I'm
going to miss that old man. I don't know why, but I
will."

"Funny world, isn't it?" I said.

And then I heard something off in the distance, a
whining noise, like a big gnat coming toward us. And
in a flash, I made a connection, remembering part of a
conversation I'd had three months ago, a detail so
small that it didn't even occur to me to write it down.

"Let's not go, just yet," I said.

Rochelle Longineau frowned. I walked over to the
shed, stood behind the wall, and watched in the direction of the lodge. The gnat sound got louder and louder
and then there it was coming toward us down the trail,
the two small headlights of an ATV.

I put my finger to my lips, and ducked behind the
wall of the shed. Rochelle Longineau followed me. We
watched as the ATV got closer and closer. Finally it

stopped, about fifty yards away from us. I strained to see who was driving the ATV, but I couldn't make them out at all, couldn't even tell if it was a man or a woman. The figure—visible only as a vague shadow—got off the ATV, came around behind the small four-wheeled vehicle, and paused. In the dim red glow of the ATV's rear lights I could only make out that the figure was winding up, throwing something into the woods.

Then Rochelle Longineau was stepping out from behind the shed with a sizable pistol and a flashlight in her hands.

"Stop!" she yelled.

But the shadowy figure was back on the ATV, still too distant to be adequately lit up in the flashlight's glow. The ATV whipped around, throwing up a shower of rock.

"Stop! Right now!"

But the ATV gathered speed and headed up the trail back toward the woods. The trail was too narrow for a car, so we couldn't give chase.

"You think we could make it going back up the dirt road and hooking back around to the lodge? Maybe get there before they leave?"

Rochelle Longineau shook her head, putting her pistol back in her purse. "Never make it," she said. "Besides, as far as the law is concerned, I'm still just a nurse. I have no legal authority to arrest anybody."

"Maybe if you radio the other cars."

"Radio's on the fritz," she said.

And then we heard a sort of thump, and a scream of pain, and the whine of the ATV suddenly went up in pitch, a brief howl, then sputtered, and died.

I started running up the trail. Rochelle Longineau followed, catching up to me in about six strides, then pulling away from me as we ran toward the two red lights that were now frozen in the middle of the trail.

When we finally stopped running, we found the ATV lying on its side. There, in the headlights in front of it, lay a deer, a big white deer, with blood streaming from its nose. Its massive, strangely twisted antlers had long been shed—but there was no doubt, this was the great white buck himself, the one the ladies at the lodge had called Moby Dick.

Rochelle Longineau swept the area with her flashlight while I stood there with my hands on my knees gasping for breath. Even over the sound of my breathing, I could hear the noise off to our left, somebody crashing through the trees. I followed the vague glow of Rochelle's white uniform.

And about a minute later we found the ATV driver, lying on the ground clutching her leg.

"I can't do it," she gasped. "I think I sprained it."

Rochelle shined the flashlight in the woman's face.

"Emily?" I said. "Emily Stubbins?"

We helped her up, supporting her on each side, took her back toward the ATV. "What a cruel irony, huh, Sunny?" she said.

"What's that?"

"Killing Moby Dick this way."

I didn't say anything.

"We need to put him out of his misery," she said. "I hate to see an animal suffer."

But when we got back to the ATV, Moby Dick was gone, nothing left but a small trail of blood drops leading off into the trees.

CHAPTER 41

"WE'RE GOING TO find it," I said, once we'd gotten into the Sheriff's Department Lincoln and started to drive. "Whatever you threw into the woods, we're going to find it."

Emily Stubbins sat there in glum silence, holding her leg, her face invisible in the darkness of the car.

"And don't try to tell me you didn't throw anything in the woods, or that you were just out here to scout for next fall's hunting season, because we all know that's crap."

Rochelle Longineau interrupted the silence, saying, "I'm taking you to the clinic in Hightower. I want to make the point to you that you're not under arrest. Matter of fact, I'm not even an officer of the law. Nevertheless, I need to inform you of your rights."

"I don't care what you do," Emily Stubbins said.

Rochelle Longineau went through the Miranda spiel.

"Why?" I said. "That's the thing I'm curious about. Was Martha blackmailing you?"

No answer.

"It was the bleach that threw us off. You killed her and then you took her shoes off and washed her feet with bleach to make it look like whoever killed her was the same person who killed Jennifer Treadaway."

Finally Emily Stubbins spoke. "I'm going to say this once, and you can do whatever you want with it. I'm going to tell you why I didn't like Martha. But then, as soon as we stop the car, I'm calling my lawyer, and after that, I suspect you won't hear a word from me."

The big car sailed through the dark pines for a while, making no sound but the huffing of the wind.

"When I told you I wasn't like those other women, Sunny," Emily said, "I wasn't kidding. All those women, they use men to get something. Even your mother, Sunny, who's more likable than most of them—for them a man is a tool, an implement, a means to an end. They see a man, they don't see an actual human being, they just see a bank account or a good name, they see comfort or ease or a means of cheap self-gratification. But me, I see a man as a completion of myself. And myself as his completion. A circle, a union, just like in some cheap romance movie—except without the complications."

"And, yet," I said, "there must have been a complication."

"When I married Bo Stubbins, we were just kids. We were both getting our Ph.D.s, both struggling to make it in a competitive little field. I didn't even know he was from a wealthy family until after we married. Had no clue. And I certainly had no way of predicting he'd become president of a major university, a big cheese in his own home town. I just married the guy because I loved him. We've been married for twenty years now and it's always been good."

Rochelle Longineau turned the Lincoln onto another

road, this one as small and dark and winding as the last.

"He's an attractive man, fun to be around, powerful—it's inevitable that women would be attracted to him. But as far as I knew, he'd always been faithful. About six months ago, though, he started acting strange. I couldn't figure out why. There were some problems at work—so I figured that was the explanation. But then, there are always problems at work. And that had never affected our relationship. But suddenly it was like I was with a stranger. He started coming home late, avoiding me—it's hard to put it into words precisely, but when you know a man inside and out and he starts acting differently, well, you know something is wrong. At first I tried to ignore it. But things got worse. I found myself picking little fights with him, pushing him away, just like he was doing to me. Bad situation. And I was starting to imagine things. Maybe he had incurable cancer, maybe this, maybe that. Finally, just as I was about to confront him, I found out the truth."

And then it was quiet for a while.

"Funny thing," she said finally, her voice suddenly sounding calmer, more professorial. "Moby Dick. That funny-looking white buck. The popular notions about female and male psychology say that women are the nurturers, men the hunters. But I'm not sure it's true. Women are hunters—it's just that we hunt men, not animals. When you think of it that way, it seems much more sinister, doesn't it?" She laughed.

"To all those women, with their bitter, grasping lives, I became a sort of reminder of what they'd given up, all of them. They hated me because they had given up love, and I hadn't. I was this constant mote in their eyes. I wasn't pretty, I wasn't grasping, I wasn't shrewd—and yet I'd ended up with this wonderful man. Whereas most of them ended up with rich jerks who treated them like dirt because they both knew the score. And a number of them got together one night, got all liquored up, and they decided they needed to take me down a peg."

"Meaning what?" I said.

"They put up a bounty, just like with Moby Dick, that funny-looking white buck. You saw that little silver cup up on the mantel in the Georgia Room, didn't you? The one that says HUNTRESS on the side? That was going to be the prize to whoever killed the white buck. So they came up with the same sort of thing: whoever could prove that my marriage was the same sort of cheap arrangement as theirs would get a little engraved silver cup."

"What did the engraving say?"

" 'Truth.' "

" 'Truth?' "

"That's it. Just 'Truth.' The idea being that it showed the real truth of what's between a man and a woman, that it's just an arrangement."

"So what happened then?"

"Martha Herrington was the one who set everything in motion. It wasn't her, of course, who actually started banging my husband. It was that horrible little Rose Ellen Knight creature. Martha Herrington gave a dinner and she sat Rose Ellen next to Bo, my husband. And Rose Ellen, she used the occasion to put on a full court press. One thing led to another."

I saw her shoulders ride up and down in the dark.

"Give Rose Ellen credit, she was a very resourceful little whore. She made films, photographs, recordings. Doing all manner of ugly, degrading things with him. It all came in the mail one day in a box with the loveliest wrapping paper. Some sort of handmade Japanese paper, carefully wrapped, nice big bow . . . It made me so sick, physically sick, I could hardly even move.

"Well, it was soon made clear to me who was behind this whole thing. I found out at your initiation ceremony. As soon as I saw that silver cup awarded to Martha, I knew what it was about. It was about all of them, and their hatred of me. I found out later in more detail. She told me herself." She laughed, a hard sound that was almost indistinguishable from a cough. "I was so naive. I thought I could be among them without being touched by them. I thought I could just go hunting down there, be polite, do my thing, and there would be no consequences to it." She laughed again.

"So, you know, I got all weird. Couldn't sleep, couldn't eat. I'd lie awake at night thinking about Martha Herrington, how much I hated her. I was practically vibrating." She rubbed her sprained knee, sighed. "And after a certain point, an idea came into my mind. An idea came into my mind and I just couldn't shake it."

"You started planning to kill her," I said.

"When we get to the clinic, I'm getting out of the car and I'm calling Quentin Senior, Jr."

I happened to be acquainted with Quentin. Notwithstanding his ridiculous name, Quentin Senior was generally recognized as the best criminal trial lawyer in Atlanta.

"I'm calling Quentin," Emily Stubbins continued,

"and then I'm closing my mouth, and that's all there is to that."

"But you did kill her," I said. "You killed her and then you took her shoes off and you washed her feet with bleach to make it look like whoever killed her was the same person who killed Jennifer Treadaway."

Emily Stubbins didn't say anything. But she didn't say I was wrong, either.

"So why her? Why not go after Rose Ellen Knight?"

"I won't answer that except to say that Rose Ellen Knight is like a cat. You don't blame her because she kills mice."

"And Martha Herrington?"

"She's not a cat. She's something else."

"I still don't understand about the knife, though," I said. "Why come back and throw it into the woods?"

No answer.

"I mean, it *was* the knife, wasn't it? That *was* what you threw into the woods, correct?"

"I won't speak to that directly," Emily said. "All I'll say is this: hypothetically, if one were to have looked for a suspect for a murder back when Martha was killed, Biggs would have seemed like a pretty good candidate. Given that we didn't know he was a fed. So making up a story about how he'd thrown something into the woods—keeping it kind of vague and soft focus—well, that would make sense, wouldn't it? So, after we talked yesterday, it occurred to me that you might actually come down here and check to see if there was anything in the woods. I mean, if you checked out my story, and it appeared that I had lied . . ." She shrugged. "Wouldn't throw me in the best light, now, would it?"

"You were about eight hours too late," I said.

The car slowed as Rochelle Longineau pulled up in front of a low brick building with a crooked sign in the front that read, WILIAMS C UNT PUB IC HE LTH.

"Well, isn't that a charmingly named place?" Emily said.

"Radical feminism arrives in Williams County," Rochelle Longineau said in her usual dry tone.

Emily Stubbins laughed. "You're gonna make a hell of a sheriff," she said. And after that, she was true to her word: she didn't even open her mouth until her lawyer arrived from Atlanta. She didn't open it after, either, for that matter.

CHAPTER 42

I ONCE BELIEVED that being a private investigator was about finding The Truth, about bringing light into the darkness. But I have come to the conclusion that it's sometimes a more nuanced business than that, that it's about finding a balance among many shades of gray. Being a private investigator is about attempting—within my narrow means—to bring unpleasant human events to some sort of closure. Generally I write a chatty, lively report. But on this one I chose to go bland and bureaucratic. Here's what I sent to Dale Herrington:

REPORT OF INVESTIGATION

SUBJECT: MURDER OF MARTHA HERRINGTON
CLIENT: DALE HERRINGTON IV
INVESTIGATOR: SUNNY CHILDS

Mr. Herrington, as per your retention letter of May 3, inst, *our firm conducted an investigation into the circumstances of your wife's death.*

Our investigation revealed three possible scenarios:

Scenario One. Uma/Horst Krens. *It is possible that your wife discovered certain facts about the drug smuggling ring conducted by Horst and Uma Krens, and that she was murdered as a result.*

Uma Krens, under a general immunity agreement with the Williams County Prosecutor and the state Attorney General, has admitted that her brother Horst killed Jennifer Treadaway in this manner. Uma admitted cleaning her feet with bleach to obliterate trace evidence of drugs.

Uma Krens, however, denies knowledge of or complicity in the murder of your wife.

One may speculate that she is lying and that the bleaching of your wife's feet, according to this scenario, was an attempt on the part of the perpetrator—presumably Uma Krens or Horst Krens—to make the two crimes resemble each other in the hopes of misleading law enforcement investigators into believing that both Jennifer Treadaway and your wife were victims of a serial killer.

While Uma's general veracity is suspect, it must be stressed that there is no direct evidence to support this scenario and we have no means of definitively refuting Uma Krens's claim that neither she nor her brother committed the crime.

Scenario Two. Dr. Emily Stubbins. *Our investigation has also revealed that Williams*

County and Georgia Bureau of Investigation personnel have recently re-interviewed an additional witness/suspect, Dr. Emily Stubbins, PhD— a member of the Hellespont Lodge. Dr. Stubbins, upon the advice of counsel, has given no statement to county authorities. While one may be tempted to make inferences from her silence, there is neither forensic nor testimonial evidence linking Dr. Stubbins directly to the crime. It is not untypical for careful defense attorneys to encourage their clients not to make statements to police.

I should add that Dr. Stubbins revealed to me that she and your wife had been engaged in a dispute of a personal nature. I can reveal the substance of that dispute to you if you wish, but I would caution you that it will not reflect particularly well on your wife's memory.

__Scenario Three. Agent Doyle Farriday, BATF.__ According to an additional statement given to me by Dr. Stubbins immediately after your wife's murder (while I was under retainer from another client), Dr. Stubbins saw Agent Doyle Farriday, an undercover operative with the Bureau of Alcohol, Tobacco and Firearms, accompanying your wife immediately prior to the murder. Additionally, she claimed to have seen him throw an unidentified object into the woods near the time of the murder.

A knife was recently discovered in the woods in the vicinity she described him having thrown the object, but DNA analysis of the knife re-

vealed nothing of value. Additionally there is reason to believe the weapon was discarded in the woods well after the murder.

Other than Dr. Stubbins's testimony, there is no evidence whatsoever connecting Agent Farriday to the knife or to the murder.

Conclusions. *No arrest has been made, and I am told by authorities that insufficient evidence is available to proceed against any suspect at this time.*

As to Scenario Three, I think we can dismiss it out of hand. Given his lack of motive and his spotless record as a law enforcement officer, I do not find Agent Farriday to be a credible suspect.

I will let Scenarios One and Two stand as I have presented them to you.

If you wish to examine the matter in further detail, I can provide you with my complete file including time sheets, witness notes, and police files.

I am sorry to leave this matter in an unresolved state, but it is my belief that further investigation into this matter will bring no definitive resolution to the case.

Witnessed this day, June 6,
[Signed]
Sunny Childs, Licensed Private Investigator
Managing Director
Peachtree Investigations

So there's truth, and there's Truth. While the omissions and hair-splitting qualifications are clear enough (you could drive a truck through "definitive resolution"), there are no flat-out lies in my statement. Whether that makes it the truth or The Truth or a big fat lie, I'll leave for you to decide.

I know the truth—small *t*. Emily Stubbins killed a woman who committed, if not a crime, then at least a vicious and unforgivable sin against her. Beyond that, I know nothing except my own yearnings for love and happiness. For whatever reason, I feel compassion for Emily Stubbins and none for Martha Herrington. But I didn't write the report the way I did in order to protect Emily Stubbins; I did it to protect Dale Herrington. He seemed like a nice man. If he chose to remember his wife as a better creature than she had actually been, maybe that was for the best.

At any rate, I never heard anything further from Dale Herrington. If he'd asked for the whole truth, I'd have told him. But he didn't ask. I like to think he'd found out precisely what he wanted to find out, no more, no less. Maybe that's wishful thinking, but that's where I'm putting it.

I saw Emily Stubbins at a lecture over at Emory a couple weeks ago. She was holding hands with her husband, Bo, and there was something grateful and sweet in their manner, like two people who had been through a terrible trial and survived.

Oh, and I might add that I took Barrington over to the mall and we looked at some china patterns. I said, "Do you think April might be a good time of the year to throw a big party? You know—old friends, relatives, people from out of state?"

And he said, "Hm. April is a nice month. April is a very nice month."

Witnessed this day,
Sunny Childs
Licensed Private Investigator

SINS OF THE BROTHER
BY
MIKE STEWART

"Chillingly believable."

—*The Washington Post*

Attorney Tom McInnes is far from nostalgic for his hometown of Cooper's Bend, Alabama. But when his black-sheep brother, Hall, is found in the river with a bullet in his neck, it's time for Tom to pay the past a visit. Greeted by the remains of his splinted family, and no satisfactory explanation for Hall's death, he realizes that he'll be staying awhile. Now, back among a few old friends and plenty of new enemies, Tom is about to uncover the kind of secrets that can turn a town—and kill a man.

"Slick, intelligent."

—*Publishers Weekly*

0-425-17887-0

TO ORDER CALL:
1-800-788-6262